James L. Fuller

The Lost Coal Mine to Oz

The Lost Coal Mine to Oz

By

James L. Fuller

Founded on and continuing the famous Oz stories by L. Frank Baum

Order this book online at www.trafford.com
or email orders@trafford.com

Most Trafford titles are also available at major online book retailers.

Printed in Victoria, BC, Canada.

ISBN: 978-1-4269-1829-2

*Our mission is to efficiently provide the world's finest, most comprehensive book publishing
service, enabling every author to experience success. To find out how to publish your book, your
way, and have it available worldwide, visit us online at www.trafford.com*

Trafford rev. 11/4/2009

 www.trafford.com

North America & international
toll-free: 1 888 232 4444 (USA & Canada)
phone: 250 383 6864 ♦ fax: 812 355 4082

Dedication

I dedicate this book to all the adults who weren't able to visit the Land of Oz as children.

Acknowledgments

I wish to thank Carolyn Owens, Violet Ogle, and Charles Stanfill for their suggestions on the plot of this story. Carolyn, Deborah Jacobs, Danny Hayes, and Violet have also helped me find many of my little errors. My wife, Ellen, deserves many thanks for her patience as I kept discussing the story with her, over and over.

Introduction

For five years, my wife and I lived in Kentucky at 261 Rocky Hollow, Raccoon. Just to be fair, the road we lived on wasn't called Rocky Hollow when we bought the house. It was called Smith Fork Road and was the hollow where the Smith's lived. Shortly after our moving there, Raccoon got 911 services and the road was renamed to Rocky Hollow because there was another Smith road in the county. Anyway, any time we tried to place a mail order by telephone, we had to wait for them to stop laughing after we gave them our address before we could complete the order.

To get to Rocky Hollow, you had to drive up three miles of narrow road called Raccoon Creek which followed the physical Raccoon Creek, (small river). At places the edge of the road had fallen into the creek. The road was just wide enough to pass a car going the other directions. It was more difficult to pass a coal truck. The approaches to some of the brides had hole in the pavement through which one could see the creek water below.

The town of Raccoon has only a Post Office and a country store.

There are family cemeteries on nearly every corner. The Smith's cemetery was up the hillside across from our home.

One winter, as we approached the bridge at the Raccoon Country Store, we had to halt for road construction. A few minutes later we saw them cart off the bridge on a very large truck. For the next three months we had to drive through the creek coming and going. Finally they returned the repaired bridge.

While we lived on Rocky Hollow, we had two flash floods go by us. Our house wasn't damaged, but the neighbors were not so lucky. Also, the road up the hollow was washed out.

Coal mines were located just about everywhere in the hills. Most people's properties had outcropping with traces of coal in them.

Three months after I wrote this book, a man showed up at the local hospital with a broken butcher knife in his back and a meat claver in his head. By the way, he survived!

Contents

Chapter 1
Spring Break

Deborah was ready for a week off from school. Her psychology students were also ready for a break. Deborah taught at an off-campus site of an Eastern Kentucky college. Her full name was Dr. Deborah Gilbert, and she was a full professor of psychology. If you traced Deborah's family tree, you will find that she had some relatives around 1900 by the names of Dorothy Gail, Uncle Henry, and Aunt Em. These relatives disappeared in the early 1900s from Kansas. Deborah liked to read and tell people about the Wizard of Oz and other Oz books.

It was time for spring break. Deborah's niece and nephew, Katie and Tommy, also had the week off from school. Tommy and Katie were coming over to spend the day with their Aunt Deborah. Their father, George, was dropping them off on his way to work. George planned to pick up Katie and Tommy again on his way home from work. The visits by Katie and Tommy always cheered up Deborah.

Tommy was a mature ten and one-half year old, who was getting involved with Boy Scouts. He liked to play all types of sports, and was really good with a computer.

Katie was a sophisticated nine and one-half year old, who was involved with Girl Scouts. She also liked cooking and thought working with computers was fun.

Deborah always had a good time when Katie and Tommy visited her. Even though this visit was just for the day, Deborah knew that she and Sigi would have a good time. Sigi was Deborah's mixed breed dog. There might even be some time to tell Katie and Tommy more Oz stories,

When Sigi started barking at the front door, Dorothy knew he wanted to go out, so Deborah went to the door and opened it for him. Sigi ran out into the front yard. Deborah followed Sigi outside. Sigi stopped, looked around and ran out to the curb. Finally, he looked down the street and barked softly.

Deborah looked in the direction that Sigi was facing. Way down the street, she could just make out a car coming toward her.

"Come now, Sigi!" remarked Deborah. "Surely, you can't tell me that you heard Katie and Tommy coming from that far away?"

"Arf, Arf!" replied Sigi, excitedly as he continued to look down the street.

As the car drew nearer, Deborah could see that it did look like the car George drove. A few seconds before the car reached Deborah and Sigi, Deborah could see that it was George, Katie, and Tommy in the car.

"Well, I'll be!" exclaimed Deborah. "I guess you can hear their car coming a long ways away. But I still find it hard to believe that your hearing is that good!"

Deborah and Sigi waited at the curb to greet Tommy and Katie. George pulled the car to the curb next to Deborah and Sigi.

Sigi said hello by barking, "Arf! Arf!" He scratched on the car door, and waged his tail.

Deborah greeted them by saying, "Hello George, Katie, and Tommy. It is always nice to see you."

"Hello, Deborah," responded George as he got out of the car and walked around to the trunk. "What a nice day for a hike."

"Hello, Auntie Deborah," said Katie and Tommy as they got out of the car and ran around to the trunk to get their things.

George opened the trunk and took out two knapsacks, two canteens and two helmets. He handed these to Tommy and Katie.

"Why do you have all of this equipment?" asked Deborah.

"You said we were going for a hike," replied Tommy, "and a Boy Scout needs to be prepared for anything."

"So do us Girl Scouts!" added Katie.

"That explains the knapsacks and canteens," agreed Deborah, "but, what are the helmets for?"

"The helmets are for protection when we ride a bicycle," stated Tommy.

"Or for when we use our roller blades," explained Katie. "Besides which, Daddy has added handless walkie-talkies to the helmets and wants us to try them out."

"That's right!" announced George. "I want Tommy and Katie to find out how far apart they can be and still talk to each other using the helmets."

"I guess Tommy and Katie can try them out on our hike," stated Deborah. "Now George, you do know where we are going to hike?"

"I believe you said that you were going to hike up the canyon beyond Opossum Bottoms," answered George.

"That's right!" agreed Deborah. "It is several miles up Pothole Creek."

"Remember, Katie and Tommy," continued Deborah, "it is always a good idea to let someone know where you are planning to go for a hike. That way, if something goes wrong, someone will know where to start looking for you."

"We'll remember that," promised Katie and Tommy together.

"Well, if you have everything," remarked George, "I think I will be getting on to work. I will return around five-thirty to pick up Katie and Tommy."

"We will be waiting for you, Daddy," called Katie and Tommy together.

"Goodbye," said Deborah. "We will see you after work."

With that, George got back into the car and drove off.

"Let's put your stuff into my car," directed Deborah, "then we just need to get my hat and my pack with the lunch in it, and we can leave."

"That sounds good to me," Tommy agreed, as he ran toward Deborah's car.

"I see you are still driving that 1960 Ford Falcon," commented Katie as she followed Tommy to the car. Sigi ran along with them.

Deborah followed along behind everyone. She unlocked the trunk of the car and Katie and Tommy placed their things in it.

Everyone followed Deborah into her house. They passed through the door, and into the living room.

"Well, let's get started on our hike!" announced Deborah. "It is a beautiful day and I can use the exercise. The weather is supposed to be in the low eighty's and sunny. However, there is a chance of thunder showers this afternoon, so we want to get our hiking in early."

"In that case," yelled Tommy, "let's get your hat and pack and be on our way."

"Arf!" agreed Sigi, who wanted to get things moving.

"Okay now! I'll get my hat from the coat rack and you two get my pack from the kitchen table," called Deborah.

With Sigi barking along behind them, Katie and Tommy ran to the kitchen to get Deborah's pack. Tommy got to the kitchen table first, and grabbed the pack. Katie, Tommy, and Sigi rejoined Deborah in the living room. Deborah got her hat from the coat rack; next, they all went out the front door of the house and headed for the car.

Deborah opened the trunk and Tommy placed Deborah's backpack in it. She closed the trunk. Deborah and Sigi got into the front seat of the car, and Katie and Tommy got into the back seat of the car.

Deborah started the car and backed out of the driveway. She headed for the four lane road leading out of town. Deborah drove north for two miles, then turned east and traveled five more miles. Here she turned right onto the Pothole Creek Road. The two lane road was very narrow with no shoulders or guard rails.

"Why do they call this Pothole Creek?" asked Tommy.

Just at that moment, Deborah bumped over several small potholes and swerved to miss two larger ones.

"Does that answer your question?" remarked Katie.

"I guess I can see where the name comes from," agreed Tommy.

"Do you want to hear the good news or the bad news first?" asked Deborah.

"What's the good news?" asked Katie.

"This is the best part of the road," stated Deborah.

"And what is the bad news?" inquired Tommy.

"After a couple miles of this," continued Deborah, "the road becomes too narrow for two lanes. Also, the potholes get worse and in some places, the edges of the road are falling into the creek."

"How far are we going on this road?" asked Katie, as she became a little scared.

"Only about three miles," responded Deborah. "It isn't too bad as long as we don't meet too many coal trucks."

"What do we do if we do meet a lot of coal trucks?" questioned Tommy, who was also fearful of the road.

"Then we have to slow down, move as far to the right as possible, and steer very carefully," stated Deborah.

Just at that moment a coal truck approached them from the opposite direction and they found out what Deborah was talking about. But they were still on the good part of the road! The coal truck came toward them at high speed with two wheels over the yellow center line. Deborah was forced to drive on the right edge of the road.

"One other thing," added Deborah, "you don't want to try passing a coal truck on a bridge or corner. There they take the whole road!"

After driving two miles, the road got narrower and there was no longer a center line. It became harder to dodge the potholes. Most of the bridges had one or more potholes in their approaches. Passing cars coming from the other direction became more challenging. Tommy and Katie became more scared as the road twisted and turned more. When no traffic was approaching from the other direction, Deborah drove down the center of the narrow road. This made it easier to dodge the bad spots in the road. Even Deborah found the drive unnerving.

Everyone was happy and relieved to hear Deborah announce that Opossum Bottoms was just around the next bend.

Chapter 2
The Hike

"I think we will park the car up there by the Opossum Bottoms Trading Post," announced Deborah, as she turned the car into the drive way leading up to the trading post. "I'll go in and ask the trading posts manager for permission to park here while we go hiking."

"We'll come with you," called Tommy and Katie, together as they quickly climbed out of the car. They were only too happy to get out of the car. It was nice to be done with the ride on Pothole Creek!

"Why not just wait in the car?" asked Deborah.

"Because I wish to make a little purchase," stated Tommy.

"He means he will buy some Big Willie's Peanut-Butter and Jelly Bars," said Katie.

"And I suppose you will buy some Malt Flavored Chocolate Balls," remarked Tommy.

"Well, if you can buy something, then I ought to be able to buy something," replied Katie. "After all, I have as many rights as you do."

"No, you don't," exclaimed Tommy. "I'm older. It gives me more rights!"

"No, it doesn't!" complained Katie.

"Okay, you two!" scolded Deborah. "Let's not argue on a nice day like this."

So Deborah, Katie, and Tommy went into the trading post to conduct their business while Sigi waited in the car with the windows rolled down.

Afterwards, they walked back to the car to get Sigi and their equipment. Then they rolled up the windows and locked the car. The four of them started hiking up the small side valley through Opossum Bottoms Hollow and beyond, following a stream. Sigi ran circles around them. He too was happy to be done with riding in the car.

Deborah, Katie, and Tommy all wore long sleeve shirts, trousers, hiking boots, and sun glasses. Deborah made sure everyone was also wearing sun block lotion. Katie and Tommy wore their helmets, and Deborah wore a straw hat.

At first there were houses built back from the creek on both sides of the creek, with a paved lane running along the left side of the creek. After they had traveled two hundred yards, the houses and lane disappeared. The lane was replaced by a dirt road. Grass, weeds, and vines grew along the road, the creek, and up the sides of the canyon.

"Now might be a good time for you two to see how well the helmet walkie-talkies work," suggested Deborah. "Why don't Tommy and Sigi go out in front of us a hundred yards or so and try them out?"

"That's fine with me," agreed Tommy.

"And then Auntie and I can catch up with you, and we will get to go on ahead," added Katie.

"Okay!" agreed Deborah. "How do you use the walkie-talkies?"

"You just turn on the switch by my right ear," explained Tommy.

"And you just listen for the other person to say something," continued Katie, "or you can say something first and then listen for the other person."

So, Tommy and Katie turned on their walkie-talkies. Tommy and Sigi ran on ahead. They were soon out of sight.

"Katie," Deborah said, "ask Tommy what he sees up ahead."

"Tommy, can you hear me?" asked Katie into her microphone. "Auntie wants to know what you see up ahead us."

"Yes, I can hear you. I see a small stream, a dirt road that is overgrown, and lots of weeds," replied Tommy into his microphone.

"Tommy says he can hear me," relayed Katie. "He sees the stream, the dirt road, and weeds." Of course, since these were handless, voice operated walkie-talkies, Tommy heard what Katie said.

"That's not what I said," interrupted Tommy. "Please try to get the message right!"

"Who asked you?" yelled Katie. "I was talking to Auntie."

"What?" asked Deborah, "I thought you were talking to me, Katie?"

"I was, but Tommy can hear everything I say to you," replied Katie.

"That's right!" remarked Tommy into his microphone. "You two have no secrets from me!"

"Tommy says we have no secrets from him," relayed Katie. "Every time I say something to you, Auntie, he hears it."

"Oh dear!" stated Deborah. "This is getting confusing. You will have to be careful about what you say. Tell Tommy to wait up for us. I think the walkie-talkies are working fine."

"Auntie says to tell you to wait up for us," repeated Katie. "She says she thinks the walkie-talkies are working fine."

"We'll wait up for you," responded Tommy, "but don't take to long."

Within a couple of minutes, Deborah and Katie had caught up with Tommy and Sigi. Tommy was sitting on a rock watching Sigi chase some butterflies.

"Tommy is there a way for you to talk to someone next to you without it going out on the walkie-talkie?" requested Deborah. "We would like to keep the walkie-talkies on but still be able to talk in, as you say, secret."

"Right!" agreed Katie. Then both Tommy and Katie jumped and tore off their helmets. The two walkie-talkies were so close together that when Katie said "Right!", it had caused feedback in the walkie-talkies and a loud shriek in both Katie's and Tommy's ears.

"Yes, there is!" answered Tommy while rubbing his ears. "You just turn off the switch that is built into the microphone like this." So Tommy showed them the microphone switch.

"That way," continued Tommy, "you can listen for the other person without them hearing what you say."

"Well, I think we will try to use that switch," suggested Deborah. "Why don't you and Sigi continue watching the butterflies, while Katie and I go on ahead a piece? When you don't hear from us every few minutes, then you are to come after us. Do you understand?"

"Yes, I understand," answered Tommy.

Deborah and Katie started walking on ahead. After each one hundred yards or so, Katie would see if Tommy could still hear her.

The walkie-talkies seemed to work well up to approximately one-half mile apart.

When Tommy didn't hear from Katie for several minutes, he and Sigi set out after Deborah and Katie. It took Tommy and Sigi about ten minutes of fast walking before they caught up with the others. They all continued on hiking together as a group. Tommy and Katie were careful to switch off the microphone switches of their walkie-talkies.

After hiking for an hour or two, they decided to stop for lunch at a meadow. Here Deborah, Tommy, and Katie took off their packs to rest. Deborah took out sandwiches and drinks for herself, Katie, and Tommy. Deborah brought dog food for Sigi. They all enjoyed lunch. Then they enjoyed eating Little Connie's Snack Cakes for dessert. Even Sigi ate one of the cakes.

After lunch they just sat around and watched the birds and butterflies that were all around them. They even saw a squirrel feeding on seeds under a bush. Everything was peaceful, and it was easy to think that no one had ever been here before them. Even though they had only hiked three or four miles, since passing the last house, it seemed like they were the only people in the whole world!

In the valley, where they were sitting, it was calm. However, there was a strong breeze blowing up near the top of the hillsides.

"Do you see those bushes up there on the hillside? When the wind blows them just right, I think I see some usual shaped white stones behind the bushes," stated Tommy. "I wonder what they are. Can we hike up there and take a look at them?"

"He's right, you know," agreed Katie. "Those stones don't look natural. I wonder what they are for, out here in the middle of nowhere."

"Well, this is your hike," announced Deborah. "So why don't you two decide. Do you want to climb up there?"

"If it is okay with Katie," stated Tommy, "we will climb up there and look at the stones as soon as we finish resting up after lunch."

"I'm with you, brother," agreed Katie, "let's do it."

So as soon as they had finished resting, they started to climb the hill up to the stones. Sigi and Tommy led the way with Katie and Deborah not far behind. The climb was harder than it looked. They were all breathing hard before they reached the top of the hill.

Chapter 3
The Hidden Graveyard

When they got near the top of the hill, they discovered that the stones were grave markers in an overgrown graveyard.

"This is an out of the way place to find a graveyard," remarked Katie.

"I guess someone must have lived out here at one time," suggested Tommy. "So I am afraid that we are not the first people to visit here."

"I don't know about you," continued Tommy, "but all the climbing makes me want a snack." So he took a Big Willie's Peanut-butter and Jelly Bar out of his pack and started to eat it.

Katie thought that a snack was good idea, so she got out a box of Malt Flavored Chocolate Balls and started eating them.

"Well, you two are still growing children, so go ahead and have a snack," puffed Deborah, as she tried to catch her breath.

"If we read some of the grave markers," continued Deborah, "they should give us the dates when these graves were made."

Tommy and Katie started reading the old head stones. "Here lies Benjamin Black, 1794-1826," read Tommy aloud. "He didn't notice that the roof was loose until it was too late. R. I. P."

"What does the R. I.P. mean?" asked Katie

"It means Requiescat in Pace, which is Latin for Rest in Peace," answered Deborah. "It was used on most of the head stones on graves of good or godly people."

"Here lies Jackie Murphy Smith, 1789-1811," read Katie. "She worked in the mine until she died of consumption. R. I. P."

"Here lies Walter Flounder, 1775-1828," stated Deborah. "He tried to dig a gold mine, but all he made was a black hole."

"It seems at that time," recalled Deborah, "that this mine was located too far out of the way to make it worth the cost of shipping the coal to the nearest coal market. About all the coal would be good for was for making hot fires for the miners."

"Here lies Daniel Potts, 1775-1804," said Tommy. "He lost his hair to an Indian hunting party. R. I. P."

"This marker is in remembrance of Joshua Smith, 1788-1810," read Deborah. "He walked into the mine one day and was never seen again."

"That's funny," observed Katie. "That stone doesn't have a R. I. P. on it."

"That's right," agreed Tommy. "Does that lack of the R. I. P. mean anything?"

"It could just be that no one thought to put the R. I. P. on the stone," remarked Deborah. "Or, since people didn't know what happened to Joshua, they didn't know if he should rest in peace."

"Here lies Ezekiel Cantrell, 1778-1822," announced Katie. "He was hung for killing two men in a fight."

"Now this person was a criminal," stated Deborah. "So people didn't wish for him to rest in peace."

"Look!" exclaimed Tommy, "there's a statue behind these big bushes. "It's a life-sized statue of a lady."

Tommy then removed several of the bushes so they could see the statue better.

"At its foot, there is a message," said Katie. "It says here lays Sarah Smith, wife of Joshua Smith, 1790-1812. She died of a broken heart two years after Joshua Smith disappeared."

"I remember hearing stories about a lost mine and graveyard," commented Deborah. "It had a statue of Sarah somebody. On nights with a full moon, the head of the statue rotates toward the lost mine. It was rumored that it was a gold mine. It sure sounds like we found the lost graveyard."

"The statue is just looking straight ahead," remarked Tommy. "When is the next night of a full moon?"

"I believe the next full moon is tomorrow night," replied Deborah.

"If we were here then, we could find the lost mine!" wished Tommy.

"Then we could all be rich!" added Katie.

While they read all the headstones, they hadn't noticed that a thunder storm was building up near them. Suddenly, there was bright lightening followed by loud thunder. It was so loud that both Tommy and Katie jumped and dropped their candy wrappers and box. Before long, it began to rain. Lightening and thunder occurred all around them. The rain increased. It was very unnerving.

"Maybe we should make a run back to the car," suggested Katie.

"I don't think that is a very good idea," advised Deborah. "Look how hard it is raining further up the valley. We don't want to be following the floor of the valley if we suddenly get a flash flood."

"What should we do?" asked Tommy. "We can't just stand here. We'll get drenched!"

Just then, Sigi started barking at a raccoon. The raccoon ran up the hill and disappeared behind some bushes. Sigi gave chase.

"Sigi, come back here!" called Tommy, as he ran after Sigi.

Katie ran after Tommy. Deborah followed everyone else.

When they got to the bushes, they noticed that there was an old mine shaft hidden behind the bushes. Nearby the shift was an old sign that showed the name of the mine as Black Hole Gold Mine. This name had been crossed out and someone had written Flounders Folly below it.

"Let's step into the old mine shaft opening and get out of this storm," said Deborah. "Maybe we can stay just inside its entrance until the storm passes?"

They stepped cautiously inside the mine shaft. The floor of the shaft was covered with a thick coat of dust and dirt. The rain increased in intensity. The little stream down below was already starting to become a big stream. Water was running off the sides of the valley into the ever enlarging stream.

"That stream looks awfully big," stated Katie.

"It looks more like a small river," noted Tommy. "And look, it is raining even harder further up the valley."

"Yes, it does!" agreed Deborah. "I am glad that we didn't try to run back down the valley."

As they continued to watch, the stream turned into a muddy roaring river. Rocks and plants along its sides were being swept down the stream.

Suddenly, Sigi started barking at something in the mine shaft. Tommy turned his Boy Scout flashlight in the direction that Sigi was looking in. There everyone saw the raccoon. It was very frightened.

The raccoon turned and started to run deeper back into the mine shaft. Before anyone could stop him, Sigi started to run after the raccoon. Tommy ran after Sigi.

"Stop, Tommy! Sigi!" called Deborah. "Come back here!"

Sigi just kept running after the raccoon.

Deborah was just able to stop Katie from running after Tommy and Sigi.

"Katie!" requested Deborah. "Call Tommy on the walkie-talkie and tell him to come back here now!"

Katie spoke into the microphone, "Tommy, can you hear me? Tommy, Auntie says for you to stop and return to us right now!"

Deborah and Katie waited for some answer on the walkie-talkie. But there was no reply.

"Try it again," said Deborah.

"Tommy!" called Katie. "You better answer us. Auntie is worried about you!" Still, there was no answer.

Meanwhile Tommy and Sigi were going deeper into the mine. The mine shift made a turn to the left. After another hundred yards, there was a side tunnel on the left. The raccoon kept running down the tunnel of the main shaft.

Another fifty yards down the main shaft, the shaft split into three shafts. This time the raccoon took the shaft on the right. Tommy and Sigi kept on following it.

"Katie, do you still have your microphone switched off?" asked Deborah.

"Oops," replied Katie, "I am afraid that I do!"

"Well turn the microphone back on and try again to call Tommy," said Deborah.

So Katie switched on the microphone and tried once more. "Tommy," said Katie, "can you hear me?"

Still, they got no reply.

Tommy thought he heard something on his walkie-talkie. He stopped and tried to give an answer. "This is Tommy," he said. "Is that you Katie?"

He got no reply.

Tommy called to Sigi, "Come back!" But Sigi just kept on chasing the raccoon. Tommy then walked a little further down the tunnel. While he was walking, he remembered that he had turned off his microphone switch.

So Tommy stopped, turned on his microphone switch, and tried to send a message on the walkie-talkie. "Katie and Deborah, this is Tommy," he called.

Katie heard a few seconds of noise on her walkie-talkie.

"Auntie!" stated Katie. "I think I hear Tommy on the walkie-talkie, but he is too far away for me to be sure."

"I guess we have no choice," decided Deborah. "We better start down the shaft toward Tommy. I hope he stays put for a few minutes."

Katie got a flashlight out of her pack. She turned it on and then Deborah and Katie started walking carefully down the mine shaft. After about one hundred yards, they came to the left turn of the shaft.

"Well this is one reason the walkie-talkies are not working so well," remarked Deborah. "They work best when you are in line of sight of each other. So after we go around this corner, why don't you try the walkie-talkie again?"

Once they rounded the corner, Katie called, "Tommy, this is Katie. Can you hear me?"

Once again, Katie listened for a reply.

There came a weak reply on the walkie-talkie, "Katie, this is Tommy."

"Auntie Deborah!" exclaimed an excited Katie, "I've got Tommy on the walkie-talkie."

"Well tell Tommy to stay put," requested Deborah.

"Tommy, this is Katie," transmitted Katie. "Auntie says for you to stay where you are."

"Okay, Katie," agreed Tommy, "I will stay where I am. Are you coming to me?"

"Tommy wants to know if we are going to him?" asked Katie.

"Tell Tommy that we are on our way," replied Deborah.

"Tommy," said Katie, "we are on our way to you. Just stay where you are."

"Okay," repeated Tommy, "I'll wait here for you. Tell Deborah that Sigi has just returned to me."

"Tommy says he'll stay put and that Sigi just came back to him," announced Katie.

"Good!" remarked Deborah. "Let's go find him before he gets too lost."

So Deborah and Katie set out after Tommy and Sigi. After carefully walking another one hundred yards, they came to a side tunnel branching off to the left. Katie shined her flashlight down the side tunnel. The tunnel only went about fifty feet before it was blocked by a pile of dirt.

"Well, I hope Tommy and Sigi didn't go that way," stated Katie.

"I don't think they did," agreed Deborah. "I don't see any foot prints leading into that tunnel."

"You are right, Auntie," observed Katie. "But there are foot prints and paw prints going down the main tunnel."

So Deborah and Katie continued down the main tunnel. After another fifty yards, the tunnel split into three tunnels.

"Okay, Katie," said Deborah, "which tunnel did Tommy and Sigi take?"

"Well, let's see," thought Katie. "There are feet and paw prints in the dirt of the right tunnel, but no prints in the middle or left tunnel. They took the tunnel on the right!"

"Very good!" acknowledged Deborah. "See if Tommy can hear us and tell him where we are."

"Tommy!" called Katie once more. "If you hear us, we are at the split of the main tunnel into three tunnels. We are taking the right tunnel."

"I think that's right," recalled Tommy. "You are coming in very loud and clear. You are almost to me."

"He says we are almost there," reported Katie.

"Yes!" exclaimed Deborah. "I think I can just make out a weak light ahead."

After walking another hundred yards or so, they met up with Tommy and Sigi.

"Well, Tommy!" began Deborah. "I wish you wouldn't run off like that. You could have gotten lost!"

"I'm sorry," apologized Tommy. "I didn't think. I was just trying to catch Sigi."

"Next time just let Sigi take care of himself," commanded Deborah. "Come on. Let's get back to the entrance before we get lost or something."

Katie asked, "What kind of something?"

"Well this is an old mine," remarked Deborah. "I estimate it to be around two hundred years old. You wouldn't want the roof to fall in on us."

"There is not much chance of that," stated Tommy with authority. "If it has been here two hundred years, it should last a few more minutes."

Chapter 4
The Cave-in

As if on a cue, they heard the mine groan about them.

"Are you sure the roof won't fall on us?" asked Katie.

"Of course I'm sure," insisted Tommy.

"Arf! Arf! Arf!" barked Sigi excitedly. He was trying to warn them that they were in eminent danger.

Deborah commanded, "Quiet, Sigi! This is no time to worry about the raccoon."

But it wasn't the raccoon that Sigi was worried about. He could hear the roof moving back up the tunnel.

Suddenly, the groan became a roar. They could hear rocks falling back up the tunnel leading toward the entrance of the mine. This was closely followed by a cloud of dust.

"I wish you hadn't said that, Tommy," coughed Katie.

"Don't blame it on Tommy," coughed Deborah. "Just save your breath! Try putting a hankie over your nose and mouth, then breathe through it. Keep your eyes shut."

The three of them sat there breathing through hankies and waiting for the dust to settle. Five to ten minutes went by before Deborah was able to open her eyes and remove the handkerchief from her face.

"Okay, everyone," announced Deborah. "You can open your eyes now!"

Katie looked at her hands and clothes. She was covered with black coal dust from head to toes. She shined her light on the others. They also were covered with coal dust. Even Sigi was all black.

"Oh Dear!" cried Katie. "We are going to get it when we get home!"

"But it wasn't our fault," stated Tommy.

"You don't think so! And who chased Sigi down into the coal mine?" asked Katie.

"But we were in the mine to get out of the heavy rain," Tommy reminded them.

"Before you worry about getting it when you get home," suggested Deborah, "let's work on getting out of here."

Immediately they started walking back up the tunnel toward the cave-in. They could only travel fifty feet.

Deborah asked Katie and Tommy shine their flashlights all around the tunnel. It was completely blocked. Most of the materials blocking the tunnel were very heavy rocks. The rocks were too heavy for Deborah, Katie, and Tommy to move. Even with Sigi helping by digging around the rocks, they still weren't able to move the rocks.

Deborah had Tommy climb up the pile of rocks and try to look between the ceiling and the rocks. He could see a small space between them, but the space was too small for him to get through. However, Tommy did feel a gentle flow of air.

"I can see a space above the cave-in," reported Tommy, "but I can't get through it. There is a flow of air going over it, so we do have air!"

Deborah remarked, "Well, this doesn't look very good. We need picks and shovels in order to clear this mess."

"Tommy," said Katie. "Surely, you have picks and shovels in your pack?"

"No!" replied Tommy. "There wasn't room for big picks and shovels in my small pack."

"Well, I thought a Boy Scout would be prepared for anything," stated Katie.

"I don't see you with any pick or shovel either," commented Tommy.

"Well, I do have a folding shovel with a small pick attachment in my pack," announced Katie. "And, I also have two rolls of bathroom tissue! It should come in handy if you should have a call of nature."

"Can we see the shovel?" requested Deborah.

"Sure!" answered Katie. She took off her pack and got out the folding shovel. Katie carefully unfolded the shovel and its pick attachment and then handed it to Deborah.

Deborah looked at the small shovel and then at the big cave-in.

"I don't think we want to dig our way out with this shovel," stated Deborah, "unless we absolutely have to!"

"If we can't clear this blockage," continued Deborah, "then we are not going to get out of the mine this way."

"So were trapped in this mine and are going to die!" exclaimed Katie.

"I should think not," Deborah assured Katie, with what she hoped was a cheerful voice. "But I do need the help of all three of you, if we are to get out of here."

"How can we help?" asked Tommy.

"Well, first we need to conserve our flashlights," suggested Deborah. "Katie, why don't you turn your light off for now?"

"Okay," agreed Katie, as she turned off her flashlight. "But I am still scared."

"It's all right to be scared," comforted Deborah, "but we have to keep our heads if we are to get out of this mess. Okay?"

"Okay," responded Katie and Tommy together.

"Tommy! Wasn't Sigi chasing a raccoon?" asked Deborah.

"Yes!" replied Tommy.

"What happened to the raccoon?" inquired Deborah.

"Why?" questioned Katie.

"Because the raccoon might know another way out of this mine," stated Deborah.

"I think the raccoon is still further down this tunnel," commented Tommy. "Maybe if we talk nicely to Sigi, he will lead us there without abandoning us this time?"

"Sigi," requested Deborah. "Can you help us to follow the raccoon while you stay with us?"

"Arf," replied Sigi. He then started walking down the tunnel with Deborah, Katie, and Tommy right behind him.

They continued to wander deeper and deeper into the depths of the earth. But all they could see was the mine tunnel that seemed to go on forever.

"It seems like we have been wandering around in this mine for days," remarked Katie.

"It has only been for a few minutes," stated Tommy. "But I think we might be lost."

"We're not lost!" insisted Deborah. "Since we haven't come across any new branches to this mine, we just have to follow our tracks back to the entrance. That is, we could if it wasn't for that cave-in."

"So, were not lost," said Katie. "We just can't get out the way we came in."

"Right!" agreed Tommy. "So since we are not lost, then what do we do?"

"We just keep exploring the mine looking for the raccoon and another way out," remarked Deborah. "We have food, water, and air. So we are in good shape. Now Sigi, let's keep following the raccoon."

So Sigi continued to lead the way and Deborah, Katie, and Tommy followed. This went on for several hours.

Eventually, the group was exhausted by all the walking, so they decided to stop for the night. Actually it was just late afternoon. Deborah had everyone eat something, though no one seemed to be very hungry. Everyone was concerned about their chances of ever getting out of the mine. Deborah decided that they should try to get some sleep. She had everyone lay down on the dry, dusty floor of the tunnel and used the back packs for pillows. They were so tired that soon everyone was fast asleep.

Chapter 5
They Meet
the Ghost of Joshua

In the middle of what they thought was the night, Sigi started to growl.

"What's wrong, Sigi?" asked a sleepy Deborah.

Sigi just kept on giving a low growl.

"Tommy," suggested Deborah, "would you turn on your flashlight and see if you can find anything wrong?"

Tommy turned on his flashlight and shined it all around the group and up and down the tunnel. Finally he said, "I don't see anything wrong, Auntie. Maybe Sigi just heard the raccoon?"

"Well there is nothing there now, so lets just go back to sleep," said Deborah.

Once again, the group went to sleep.

A few minutes passed without any more problems. Then Sigi started growling again.

"Sigi!" commanded Deborah, "Be quiet!"

Sigi stopped growling.

Just at that moment everyone heard a howling noise.

"Sigi!" called Deborah.

Sigi responded, "Arf!" But the howling noise was heard at the same time.

Once more, Deborah had Tommy turn on his flashlight and look all around. There was still nothing there! At this point, the batteries in Tommy's flashlight started to fail.

"That's okay, Tommy," Deborah assured him. "We won't need your light for the rest of the night. So let's just go back to sleep and figure out what to do in the morning."

So once again everyone tried to go back to sleep.

Then Sigi started to growl again, and the howling noise was heard more loudly. But this time, Katie also saw a faint glowing cloud moving about back up the tunnel.

"Auntie!" called a startled Katie. "What is that faint light moving about there? Is it a ghost?"

"Don't be silly," stated Tommy. "Everyone knows that there are no such things as ghosts!"

"Besides!" added Deborah with what she hoped was a reassuring voice. "If that's a ghost, it must be sick! It couldn't scare anyone!"

The groan turned into a "bu-uu-tt, bbu-uu-tt, bbu-ut-tt!" The faint moving light blinked with each uttered sound.

"You are going to have to do better than that," said Katie bravely.

"Perhaps if you were to shine a little brighter?" suggested Tommy.

"Or take on some scary form," advised Deborah. "Frankly, you are a poor imitation of a ghost! You can't scare us. You just make us laugh."

With that, Deborah started laughing and signaled Katie and Tommy to laugh as well. This finally got the response of, "You-uu are terrible people!" from the faint moving light. But at least the voice was getting clearer.

"And why are we terrible?" asked Deborah.

"Why you are laughing at me!" answered the voice. "Is that any way to treat a ghost? Even if I haven't had any practice for nearly two hundred years."

"Can you shine a little brighter and show us what you look like?" requested Katie.

"Give me a moment or two," replied the voice. "I think I can remember how make myself appear."

In a few moments, the faint moving light became much brighter and it started to take on the form of a man. "How's this?" asked the figure.

"That's much better," remarked Deborah. "I think you look like a man of some kind. I'm sure that with a little more practice, you will be able to give us a clear form!"

"I'm trying," stated the figure. "I think I'm getting my voice back and I am getting better at showing my form."

"Yes," agreed Katie, who was no longer scared; instead she was becoming very curious. "By the way, I think you are bright enough to be used as a light for us."

"Now just you hold on there," replied the form that was looking much more like a human form. "We ghosts or spirits have our pride! Let's not get too friendly, too quickly."

"Perhaps you could start by telling us who or what you are?" asked Deborah. "That is, if you are strong enough to do so?"

The spirit said, "I am the ghost of Joshua Smith. I was murdered in 1810, and you will found my body buried at the end of the first side tunnel on the left."

"So why are you haunting us?" requested Tommy. "We haven't done anything to you!"

"Have you looked around much?" questioned Joshua. "Who else is there for me to haunt. Besides, as a ghost, I am required to haunt people until I get justice."

"And when will justice be done?" inquired Tommy.

"Why justice will be done when those who murdered me are brought to trial and my name is cleared. That will allow me to go to my eternal rest," stated Joshua.

"We didn't murder you," remarked Deborah. "Wouldn't it work better if you haunted the guilty persons until they confess?"

"Well, that's what I am supposed to do," replied Joshua. "But I have a problem. The guilty persons have been dead for almost two hundred years. So the best I can do is to get someone to prove that I was murdered, and by whom."

As the ghost continued to talk, its form became that of a man from the early 1800s. It continued to grow brighter and clearer with time.

"Right!" exclaimed Katie. "Meanwhile, you are going to kill all of us."

"I am a spirit," repeated Joshua. "I cannot move physical things or hurt living people. Well, that is, I can scare people a little."

"It seems like you are scaring all of us," remarked Deborah. "Perhaps if we thought that you could help us, then we could help you."

"I don't understand," replied the spirit.

"Well," said Tommy, "we are trapped in this coal mine. Can you help us to get out of it?"

"Now I understand," said the spirit of Joshua. "If I can be kind to you, then you will try to help me."

"Only if you don't scare us to death first," Katie reminded him. "I am afraid that we haven't had much experience with spirits. But from your appearance, I don't think it will be too hard to prove that you were murdered."

By now Joshua's form showed that he had a hatchet stuck in his head and a knife sticking out of his back.

"Okay," agreed the spirit of Joshua. "Let's start over. Hello. My name is Joshua Smith. Why don't you just call me Joshua? I died in this mine in 1810."

"Very well," answered Deborah. "I am Deborah Gilbert. This is my niece, Katie. This is my nephew, Tommy. And this is my dog, Sigi. We have been trapped in this mine by a cave-in. Do you know another way out of the mine?"

"I am not sure," responded Joshua. "As a ghost, I am not allowed to leave the mine area. I mean that I can't go outside the mine entrance."

"Do you know what is down this tunnel?" requested Deborah. "Or perhaps you know where the raccoon, that started all our problems, has gone?"

"Actually," stated Joshua, "I haven't had any reason to go much further into the mine than this."

"Maybe Joshua could see how bad the cave-in is?" suggested Katie.

"And how is he to do that?" asked Tommy.

"Well, can't ghosts go through walls and things?" replied Katie.

"I do think you have an idea there," agreed Tommy.

"Joshua!" asked Deborah. "Can you move through these rock walls?"

"Yes!" replied Joshua. "What did you have in mind?"

"Do you know where the cave-in is near the start of this tunnel?" continued Deborah.

"I can find it easy enough," answered Joshua.

"Can you determine how big the cave-in is? Maybe you can look at the cave-in from both sides?" continued Deborah.

"Yes, I think I could do that," said Joshua.

"Good!" remarked Deborah. "That's the first thing you can do for us. While you are gone, the rest of us will try to get some sleep. We can also think about how we are going to help you."

So Joshua went off to look over the cave-in, while Deborah, Katie, Tommy, and Sigi got some more sleep.

When Joshua reached the cave-in, he looked at it from the inside and the outside. He even squeezed his way through the space between the old ceiling and the pile of caved-in rocks. Afterwards he made his way back to Deborah and her friends. While Joshua could have made this trip very quickly, he instead decided to take several hours so that Deborah and the others could get more rest.

It was about eight o'clock when Joshua finally woke up Deborah, Katie, Tommy, and Sigi. Everyone assumed that it was morning. Actually it was just eight in the evening. When tripped in a dark mine, one soon losses track of time.

"Good morning!" announced Joshua. "It's time to get up."

"Can you throw a little more light on your form?" requested Katie. "I still find this mine very dark."

So Joshua turned up the power on his ghost image.

"That's better," said Tommy. "Wait until I tell the other Boy Scouts about using a ghost for a flashlight!"

"Okay, now everyone," declared Deborah, "why doesn't Joshua tell us what he found out about the cave-in, while the rest of us have something to eat. As a ghost, Joshua, I assume you do not eat?"

"No, I don't eat!" stated Joshua. "Eating would require that I could move physical objects. So don't mind me, you just go ahead and eat without me."

"Do you have any hot oatmeal in your pack, Auntie?" asked Tommy. "That is what I usually have for breakfast."

"I am afraid not," said Deborah, "but I do have some trail mix, dried fruit, and fruit juice. That should make a good breakfast."

"That sounds good to me, too!" added Katie. "I'm so hungry that I could eat a horse."

So Deborah, Katie, Tommy, and Sigi sat down and started eating while Joshua began telling about the cave-in.

"The top of the rock pile blocking the tunnel has room above it for you to climb over the pile," began Joshua. "However, where the pile goes above the tunnel roof, there isn't more than six inches of space. The dog might be able to get through there, but the rest of you are too big to get through that space. The rocks on this side of the pile are too heavy for you to move. You would need picks and shovels to break the rocks into smaller pieces. Do you have picks and shovels?"

"Katie has a small folding shovel," replied Deborah, "but it is too light a tool to do the job."

"In that case," stated Joshua, "I don't think you can get past the cave-in. Some one would have to dig you out from the outside."

"So, we can wait at the cave-in for a rescue that may not come," remarked Deborah, "or we can see if we can find another way out."

"What if someone tries to dig us out while we are elsewhere in the mine?" asked Tommy.

"Then they will have to follow our tracks until they catch up with us," responded Deborah.

Chapter 6
The Underground Lake

"So, when do we start looking for another exit?" asked Katie.

"We started looking for another exit yesterday," said Deborah. "We can continue our search as soon as we finish breakfast."

Everyone, except Joshua, went back to eating their breakfast. Within a few minutes, everyone had finished eating. Next, they gathered up everything and got ready to start moving again.

"Sigi! Are we still following the raccoon?" asked Deborah.

"Arf!" said Sigi, as a yes.

"Okay, now Sigi," directed Deborah, "you lead the way, but don't run away and leave us."

"Arf!" replied Sigi, and started walking and sniffing his way down the tunnel.

Joshua, with his glowing image, was right behind Sigi. Everyone else followed close behind.

The tunnel was slowly curving to the left. The group had traveled for about fifteen minutes when they heard Sigi start barking. It appeared that Sigi had reached the end of the tunnel. He was barking and looking at a hole on the right side of the tunnel. The hole was a foot to a foot and one half in diameter.

"Well now," remarked Tommy, "I think Sigi has found the raccoons hiding place."

"That's fine," stated Katie, "but I think we have run out of tunnel to explore."

Sigi started to enter the hole.

"Hold it, Sigi!" commanded Deborah. "You stay here with us for now."

"Arf!" responded Sigi, and came and stood by Deborah.

"Whether we have run out of tunnel to explore or not depends on where that hole leads to," continued Deborah.

"You're not thinking of us crawling through that hole, are you?" questioned Katie. "My cloths are in bad enough shape without doing that."

"A good scout should be willing to do whatever is necessary!" announced Tommy. He then started to crawl into the hole.

"Hold it Tommy!" called Deborah. "I don't think you should do that yet. We have a better way to explore the hole."

"We have?" asked Tommy.

"Of course we have!" stated Katie. "We have Joshua. He can explore the hole without any risk. After all, he is already dead!"

"Joshua!" said Deborah. "Would you mind exploring this hole for us? We would like to know if it goes anywhere, and if we can get through it?"

"That should be easy enough for me to do," agreed Joshua. "I don't see any reason why I shouldn't do it, so I'll do it for you. Give me a few minutes to see what I can find out."

So Joshua went into the hole. The further he got into the hole, the darker the main tunnel became.

"Should I turn on my flashlight?" asked Katie. "Or should we just wait here in the dark?"

"You're not afraid of the dark are you?" teased Tommy.

"Girl Scouts are not afraid of the dark," said Katie with a shaky voice. "When we have camp-outs, we sit around the campfire at night and tell ghost stories."

"Well, you should have a good ghost story to tell when you go on your next camp-out," remarked Deborah, with a hopefully cheerful voice. "I think we will save the flashlight for later. Let's just wait and talk in the dark until Joshua returns."

"Well, I, for one, am glad to see you two ladies are not afraid of the dark," stated Tommy.

"It's all right to be afraid of things, Tommy," said Deborah. "But don't let those things control you. Brave people can be afraid like any other persons. It's just that they do what needs to be done in spite of their fears."

"So it's okay if I am a little bit afraid?" asked Katie. "I don't know how we are going to get out of this mine."

"That problem has me a little bit scared," admitted Tommy. "But I am sure Auntie has it all figured out."

"Do you know how we will get out of this mine, Auntie?" requested Katie.

"Well, I am working on that problem," responded Deborah. "I hope that Joshua will have some good news for us when he gets back."

The discussion by Katie, Tommy, and Deborah continued for several more minutes. They were so engrossed in their discussion in the dark that they soon forgot about Joshua. It was only when a light started glowing from the hole that they remembered him.

"Auntie!" announced Katie. "I think Joshua is returning. The hole is glowing!"

"Good!" stated Tommy. "It will be nice to see his light again!"

By now, everyone was watching the hole. It was giving off more light all the time. Finally, Joshua was once again in the main tunnel.

"Hello," greeted Joshua. "Did you miss me?"

"Yes, we missed you!" said Katie.

"What news do you have for us?" asked Tommy.

"Well, I was able to explore hole," replied Joshua. "It goes back about one hundred feet and then comes out in a very large cave. I didn't see the raccoon, but I think it went through the hole and into the cave. Oh! And I also heard the sound of falling water."

"But is the hole big enough for us to get through?" inquired Deborah.

"I think you can crawl though the hole if you are careful," responded Joshua. "Tommy or Katie should lead the way with the little shovel. They could use it to enlarge the narrower spaces in the hole."

"I think I should go first with the shovel," remarked Tommy.

"I think I should go first with my shovel," stated Katie.

"But I am bigger and stronger," insisted Tommy.

"But it is my shovel!" cried Katie.

"I think you two should stop fighting," scolded Deborah. "We will have Joshua go first and light the way. We will have Tommy go second and use the shovel to make the hole bigger. Then Katie will follow with Sigi in between her and Tommy. Katie can use her flashlight to help her and I see where we are going. Both of you will have work to do. I will bring up the rear. Are there any questions?"

"No!" answered Katie and Tommy together.

"Okay, everyone!" commanded Deborah. "Let's get started."

So Joshua led the way into the hole. Tommy got the shovel from Katie and followed Joshua. Sigi came next. Katie got out her flashlight and climbed into the hole after Sigi. Finally, Deborah squeezed her way into the hole and carefully followed the others.

Joshua and Tommy moved slowly so everyone could keep up. Tommy was able to crawl through most of the hole on his hands and knees. He stopped several times to enlarge narrow places in the hole.

Sigi had no problem at all walking through what he considered to be a large hole. He couldn't imagine why the others were having trouble getting through the hole.

Katie was also able to crawl through the hole on her hands and knees. She stopped every so often to shine the flashlight in Deborah's direction.

Deborah's passage through the hole was quite an ordeal. There wasn't room for her to crawl on hands and knees. She had to do more wiggling than crawling. She would stretch out to her full length and then try to bring her body and legs forward. Next she would stretch out again. It was a slow process. She wouldn't have made it through the hole without Tommy's work with the shovel.

Finally after fifteen long minutes, Deborah was helped out of the hole by Katie and Tommy.

"Well, that wasn't so bad," remarked Tommy.

"True," added Katie, "and I think we are in a big cave." She then shined her flashlight around. However, the cave was so big, that she was only able to see a little section of it and a lot of open space.

"That's fine, for you little people!" complained Deborah as she started to bush off her clothes. "But I just barely managed to get through that hole and I kept hitting my head on the ceiling. I hope we don't have to go back through that hole again!"

"I don't know about you" announced Katie, "but my clothes need washing and I could use a bath!"

"My clothes could use some help too," agreed Tommy.

"My hat is ruined!" stated Deborah. "My hair is full of dirt! Joshua! Didn't you say you heard falling water?"

"Yes! I said I heard falling water," recalled Joshua. "Listen!"

So everyone was quiet for a moment. Then they were able to hear a waterfall.

"I hear it!" exclaimed Tommy.

"But where is it?" asked Katie.

"Joshua!" requested Deborah. "Why don't you go see if you can find the water?"

"Okay!" agreed Joshua. "I'll be back in a few minutes. Don't go away."

So Joshua went looking for the water, while Deborah, Katie, and Tommy talked to each other in the dark.

"Katie!" said Deborah. "Why don't you turn your flashlight on and see which way the raccoon went?"

So Katie turned on her flashlight. She and Tommy looked for tracks all around them. On their left, they found raccoon tracks.

"So now we know which way the raccoon went," remarked Deborah. "Now turn off the flashlight. Then we will just wait for Joshua to return."

Within a few minutes, Joshua returned.

"Well now! Hi again," called Joshua. "Perhaps I can throw some light on the subject of where the waterfall is located."

"So where is it?" asked Katie.

"First I better tell you where you are," stated Joshua.

"Why?" questioned Tommy.

"You are in a dangerous place! If you should decide to take a short walk in the dark," replied Joshua, "you would be in for a big fall. And I do mean a BIG FALL!"

"What? I don't understand," said Deborah.

"At present, you are all standing on a wide cliff!" continued Joshua. "If you walk off the edge of the cliff then you are in for a thirty foot or so fall! And then you would probably end up in the lake!"

"We're on a cliff!" stated Tommy.

"There's a lake thirty feet below us!" exclaimed Katie.

"But the lake isn't making the sound of falling water, is it?" asked Deborah.

"No!" answered Joshua. "The lake isn't making the falling water sound. The sound is being made by a waterfall on your left, about one hundred and fifty feet further along this cliff."

"What are we waiting for?" requested Katie. "Here is our chance to wash up!"

"And it is the direction that the raccoon took!" added Tommy.

Chapter 7
The Waterfall

Joshua led the way to the waterfall. Here, Deborah, Katie, Tommy, and Sigi got a chance to wash some of the dirt off of themselves.

Since Sigi was a dog, he simply ran back and forth through the waterfall. When he was finished, he shook himself dry. This got everyone near him all wet.

Katie got a small bar of soap and a hand towel out of her pack and was soon busy washing her face and hands. Next she got down on her knees and leaned her head under the waterfall. She applied soap to her hair. Finally, she rinsed her hair in the waterfall and dried it with her towel. She felt much better.

Deborah duplicated the actions of Katie. Once again, Deborah was glad she had had her hair cut short. It really made washing it easier.

Poor Tommy had to wait while the ladies were washing up. He tried to wash his hands and face using just the water, but he didn't come clean.

"How come Sigi comes clean with just water?" asked Tommy. "But I don't?"

"Because Sigi is semi-self-cleaning," stated Deborah, "but you're not! Maybe you can borrow some soap when Katie and I are finished."

Finally, after Deborah and Katie were finished washing up, Katie offered Tommy the use of her Girl Scout soap! Next time, Tommy would have to remember to pack a bar of soap.

During all of this time, Joshua kept his ghostly light shining so everyone could see what they were doing. His image wasn't dirty, and even when he did pass through the waterfall, it didn't get him wet.

"Well now!" said Deborah. "I sure feel better for the chance of washing up a little."

"Yes!" agreed Tommy. "I guess it does feel good to be clean once in a while."

"Now if we only had a washing machine," remarked Katie. "My clothes still need a lot of work."

"Perhaps we can do something about our clothes a little later," suggested Deborah. "But first, Joshua, can you find us a way down to the lake?"

"It will take a little while," replied Joshua. "I'll need to explore the cliff in both directions."

"Just fine!" stated Katie. "And I guess we will all just wait in the dark again!"

"That all depends," said Deborah. "Tommy and Katie, did either of you think to bring along spare batteries for your flashlights?"

"Now I'm sure that a Girl Scout who remembered to bring along bathroom tissue, shovel, and soap, must have remembered to bring spare flashlight batteries!" commented Tommy.

"Actually, I did"" announced Katie. "I do have a spare set of batteries for my flashlight! What about you, brother?"

"Now that you mention it," continued Tommy, "I did bring along <u>two</u> sets of spare batteries for my flashlight. So There!"

"Okay, you two"" exclaimed Deborah. "You are both good scouts. Now if Tommy will just change the batteries in his flashlight before Joshua goes off searching for a path to the lake, then we will not have to sit here in the dark!"

So Tommy got a set of spare batteries out of his pack and placed them in his flashlight. He then placed the used batteries back in his pack. After all, a good scout doesn't litter!

So Joshua set off to find a way down to the lake, and Tommy shined his light around the waterfall.

"I wonder what happened to the raccoon?" asked Tommy. "I see its tracks all around this side of the waterfall."

"Maybe it crossed to the other side of the waterfall?" suggested Katie.

"I don't think so," remarked Deborah. "There are an awful lot of tracks on this side of the waterfall. It looks like the raccoon kept walking up and down searching for something. Sigi, do you think you can find the raccoon?"

"Arf! Arf!" replied Sigi and he started sniffing all around. After a moment or two, Sigi walked up to the very back of the waterfall and growled softly.

Deborah, Katie, and Tommy went over to where Sigi stood.

"Tommy!" called Deborah. "Can you shine your flashlight back behind the waterfall?"

"Sure!" agreed Tommy and he shined his flashlight behind the waterfall.

About ten feet back under the waterfall, they saw two shining eyes.

"I think I have found the raccoon," remarked Tommy, "and it looks like it is very scared!"

"Sigi!" commanded Deborah. "Come back away from there, and do stop growling."

Sigi made a soft, "Arf!", and came over to Deborah.

"Tommy!" suggested Katie. "Let's all go back to where we washed up and leave the poor raccoon alone."

"Okay!" agreed Tommy, reluctantly.

They all went back to where they had washed up.

"I wish we could make friends with the raccoon," stated Tommy.

"What if we were to leave a little food up there?" commented Katie. "I don't think the raccoon has eaten since it ran into the mine."

"How about it, Auntie?" asked Tommy.

"Well, I guess we can spare a little food," replied Deborah. She then looked in her pack. "Would some dried fruit do?"

"That will do fine!" said Tommy. He took the fruit and placed it toward the back of the waterfall.

"Now we just need to stay away from there and wait and see what happens," suggested Katie.

"And Sigi," commanded Deborah, "you need to be really quiet. Okay!"

Sigi gave a soft whine in agreement.

About this time, Joshua returned.

"Hello again!" greeted Joshua. "Did you miss me?"

"No!" replied Deborah. "We've been busy finding the raccoon. However, since you are back, what did you find out?"

"I looked for a path down to the lake in both directions," reported Joshua. "The cliff on the right ends about one hundred feet past the hole you came through. However, on the other side of the waterfall, the cliff goes on for about two hundred more feet. At its end, there is a narrow path leading down to the lake."

"So, we have to cross the waterfall in order to get down to the lake!" remarked Katie.

"That's right," agreed Joshua.

"What are we waiting for?" inquired Tommy. "Let's get going."

"I think it is about lunch time," stated Deborah. "Why don't we eat before we try to cross the waterfall and go down to the lake?"

Actually it was just eleven-thirty at night.

This sounded like a good idea to Katie, Tommy, and Sigi. Joshua didn't need food, nor could he eat food. So Joshua just sat quietly while the others ate lunch.

"How is the raccoon doing?" asked Katie to no one in particular.

Tommy shined his flashlight toward the back of the waterfall. There by the dried fruit was the raccoon. He turned his flashlight off.

"It appears that the raccoon is more hungry than scared," announced Tommy. "Can I toss a little more food toward it?"

"I don't see why not," agreed Deborah, and she got some more dried fruit from her pack.

Tommy tossed the fruit about half way between them and the raccoon.

"We can check on that fruit in a few minutes," recommended Katie. "But I think you may be making a new friend, Tommy."

"Okay, gang! How do we get across this waterfall?" asked Deborah.

"Well, we can just try to walk across the falls at the edge of this cliff," suggested Katie.

"Or we can just try to go behind the waterfall," added Tommy. "That is, if the raccoon doesn't object?"

"I don't think the raccoon will mind," observed Deborah. "If you turn your head really slowly and look behind you, I think you will see your new friend, Tommy."

Tommy carefully turned his head and looked down. There was the raccoon looking up at him.

"I must assume that neither path will be easy," stated Deborah. "Otherwise, the raccoon would have crossed the waterfall in order to get away from us."

"Well, I for one think the path along the cliff edge is too dangerous," decided Katie. "Let's look behind the falls."

So Joshua led the way and everyone walked to the back of the falls. Sigi and the raccoon brought up the rear. Joshua went on across behind the waterfall and returned.

"It looks like it is possible to get through from behind the waterfalls," announced Joshua. "Since I can't touch things, I can't be sure how slippery the rocks are."

"Well, there is one way to find out," suggested Tommy, and he started to cross behind the falls.

"Hold it!" commanded Deborah. "Before we get started, let's make sure our packs are sealed water tight!"

The three of them checked that everything in their packs was protected from the possibility of water getting into their packs. They were ready to cross the waterfalls.

Joshua floated above the group. Tommy started working his way behind the falls. The going was slow, as he carefully moved from one slippery rock to another. Katie followed Tommy. Deborah came last. They held onto each other.

As the group moved slowly across behind the waterfall, Katie lost her footing on the rocks.

"Help!" cried Katie as her feet slipped off the rocks and into the cold water.

"Don't worry!" Deborah assured her. "Tommy and I have got hold of you."

Tommy and Deborah tried to pull Katie back up on the rocks. But they were not able to do so.

"Perhaps if we move a little further across the falls," suggested Tommy, "we may then find some rocks for Katie's feet. Then it should be easier to get her back up!"

"Good idea," agreed Deborah. So Deborah and Tommy inched their way further across the falls pulling Katie with them. By now, Deborah was standing on the slippery rocks that Katie had fallen from.

"Okay," called Tommy, "on the count of three, we will pull you back up!"

"I am ready!" agreed Katie. "I think my shoes have been washed enough!"

So Tommy counted to three and both he and Deborah pulled hard together. They almost had Katie back onto the rocks when Tommy lost his footing and slipped off the rocks. Deborah tried to hold up both Tommy and Katie, but then she lost her footing too.

"Oh no!" shouted Tommy as he slid down the waterfall, across the cliff, and down to the lake.

"Help!" cried Katie, as she followed Tommy.

"Oh my!" called Deborah as she, too, went over the cliff edge.

Chapter 8
The Visit to the Lake

The three of them splashed down into the lake thirty feet below. They bobbed to the surface. Two more splashes were heard behind them. Shortly there after, Joshua floated above them.

"This is entirely your fault, Katie!" remarked Tommy. "You wanted to wash your clothes."

"I wanted to wash them in a washing machine," exclaimed Katie, "not in the lake."

"Let's stop the fighting and get ashore." suggested Deborah. "Joshua shows us the way to shore?"

So Joshua lit the way to the shore and everyone followed his lead. Shortly, Deborah, Katie, Tommy, Sigi, and the raccoon were sitting on the shore.

Sigi and the raccoon shook themselves dry. The people were not as fortunate as the animals.

"Burrr!" said Katie. "I'm cold!"

"And I am wet all over," added Tommy.

"We need to get dried out!" stated Deborah. "Was I mistaken, or did I see a light far off to the left as we were falling?"

"I think I saw something," said Katie.

"Me too!" agreed Tommy.

"We should check that out," announced Deborah, "but first let's try and start a fire and get warm. While we are doing that, we will have Joshua see what that light is."

So Katie and Tommy looked in their packs for matches and Deborah looked around for something that might burn.

Katie found some matches. Tommy found some pieces of paper. Deborah found some small sticks and some lumps of coal. Within a few minutes, they had a small fire burning. Deborah, Katie, and Tommy sat around the fire and warmed themselves.

Meanwhile, Joshua left the group and went to see what was causing the light far down the lake. While he was gone, everyone else busied themselves with getting dry. This took a couple of hours.

"Wow!" exclaimed Katie. "That slide down the waterfall was kind of fun!"

"Yeah, it was great!" added Tommy. "Auntie, can we try that slide again?"

"No!" answered Deborah. "Only one ride to a customer! Beside, no one got hurt this time, but who can say that we will be so lucky next time."

"If the raccoon is going to stay with us," suggested Katie, "shouldn't it have a name?"

Tommy suggested, "How about Beggar? It does seem to be willing to beg food off us."

Deborah countered with, "I think Rocky would be a good name. After all, we found it in the rocks."

"Rocky sounds nice," agreed Katie and Tommy.

"Hello, Rocky!" greeted Tommy. "My name is Tommy."

"And I am Katie," added Katie.

"I am Deborah!" said Deborah. "And this is Sigi."

About the time everyone was feeling comfortable again, Joshua returned. He wasn't looking all that happy.

"Hello! Joshua!" said Deborah. "Did you find the source of the light?"

"Yes, I did!" replied Joshua. "There is a small amount of volcanic action about half a mile down the lake shore. You saw a small flow of lava. It gives off light and heat."

"You don't look very happy," observed Katie.

"What's the matter, Joshua?" asked Tommy. "Is the volcano about to explode?"

"No! The volcano is quiet enough," responded Joshua. "And I have been gone closer to two hours. I have been all around the lake and can't find any way out of here!"

"So, you will have to take a second look around the lake and cave," suggested Deborah. "But first, why don't you lead the way to that warmth and light-giving volcano?"

First Katie and Tommy drowned the fire with water. Once that was done, Joshua led the way along the lake shore and Tommy, Katie, Deborah, Sigi, and Rocky the raccoon, followed behind him in a single file. The shore line was very rocky and progress was slow.

After much work, the party arrived at the site of the volcano. The volcano gave off enough light so that Joshua's image made no difference on the ability of everyone to see things.

"This is great!" exclaimed Deborah. "That trip was harder than it looked, but we now have light, warmth, and all the water we can drink. Maybe Tommy can try fishing in the lake later."

"Of course, Tommy can go fishing," commented Katie, "if he remembered to pack a fishing pole!"

"I have fish hooks, line, and lures in my survival kit," stated Tommy. "If we were along a creek then I could have cut a pole from some of the trees or bushes!"

"I have a telescoping pole," Katie announced proudly. "I'll let you use it for a small consideration!"

"How about you get to eat some of the fish?" suggested Tommy.

"I guess that'll have to do," answered Katie as she handed Tommy the pole.

"That's fine!" agreed Deborah. "You two can go fishing while Joshua looks around and above the lake!"

So Katie and Tommy went looking for a good place to fish. Sigi and Rocky followed them. Meanwhile Joshua set out to look over the entire lake and cave. Deborah found a comfortable rock and took a short nap.

An hour or so later, everyone returned to where Deborah was napping.

"Wake up, Auntie!" called Tommy, as he shook her.

"Look what we caught!" announced Katie.

Deborah asked, "Who? What? Where am I?"

"You are in a large cave with a lake and volcano in it," Joshua reminded her.

"Oh yes!" answered Deborah. "For a moment there, I thought it was all a dream! Well, back to reality. So what did you catch, Katie?"

"Why, we caught some fish!" replied Katie.

"With a little help from Joshua," added Tommy. "He's not only a good fish finder, but he can also scare the fish onto the fish hook!"

"Excellent!" agreed Deborah. "I guess dinner is on Joshua. Thank you, Joshua!"

Dorothy looked at her watch. It said four-thirty. Dorothy thought it was later afternoon. It was really early morning.

"I'm glad that I could do something helpful," replied Joshua, "but you may not like my report."

"Well! Let's eat dinner first," suggested Deborah, "then you can give your report."

"Auntie!" said Katie. "How are we going to cook the fish?"

"We don't need to cook it!" remarked Tommy. "We just eat it raw! Haven't you ever heard of sushi?"

"Oh! Yuck!" cried Katie.

"Why don't we boil the fish in that hot water pool over there?" suggested Deborah. "That is unless Tommy objects."

"Boiled fish sounds okay to me!" responded Tommy.

"That's fine!" said Deborah. "We can use some of the fishing line to hold the fish while it cooks."

"But first we need to clean the fish," stated Katie. "Anyone got a knife?"

"Why not use the knife in Joshua's back?" suggested Tommy.

"Well that knife is just an image like the rest of me," replied Joshua. "It would only be good for cleaning ghosts of fish!"

"Katie! Do you have a knife?" asked Dorothy.

"No, I don't," answered Katie. "Do you have one, Tommy?"

"Well, I do have my Boy Scout knife!" replied Tommy. He handed the knife to Deborah.

So Deborah and Katie took the fish down to the lake shore and cleaned them, next they cooked the fish in the hot water pool. Everyone sat down and ate the fish, along with some other things from Deborah's pack. Even Sigi and Rocky joined in eating the fish.

When everyone was finished eating, Deborah asked Joshua for his report.

"My report is simple," began Joshua. "We are in a large cave with a lake and volcano in it. The only ways in and out of the cave, except for the hole we came through, are an underground river and air vents high up in the roof. The vents are only an inch or so in size."

"Joshua, you are saying that the only way for us to get out of here is back through the mine entrance?" asked Deborah

"That's about it," agreed Joshua.

"Well, at least we have light, warmth, food, water, and air," remarked Tommy. "This could be a great adventure!"

"I, for one, have had enough adventure," stated Katie. "I want to go home."

"And I want you to get out of here so you can get me justice!" said Joshua.

"Someone should be out looking for us," Deborah assured them. "What we need to do is to decide whether to stay here or go back to the cave-in, but that can wait until morning. Let's all get some sleep."

With that, everyone found a comfortable place to rest and went to sleep. Everyone was dreaming about different things that they would do once they were out of the mine.

Deborah did not rest very well. She was concerned with what would be the right thing for them to do. Should they stay here at the lake or should they go back to the cave-in?

After all, they were in a "Lost Mine!" What chance was there that anyone would find them?

Chapter 9
The Party is found
by Nomes

"Wake up! Wake up!" called some nomes to Deborah, Katie, Tommy, Rocky, and Sigi. "Do you intend to sleep all day?"

Now being woken up by a nome can be a shock to a human. After all, nomes are short, fat creatures with hair all over their bodies including long beards.

"We must hurry," stated the Nome Leader. "The Nome King is expecting you. You know how he is when he is kept waiting."

A scared Katie cried, "Who? What are you?"

"Where did you come from?" asked an equally startled Tommy.

"We are nomes or underground fairies. I am Captain Mudd," replied Nome Leader. "The Nome King sent us for you."

"You mean nomes like those nomes mentioned in the Oz stories?" asked Deborah, who still didn't think she was awake.

"Yes!" responded the Nome Leader. "We are nomes like those mentioned in the books about the Land of Oz. Wake up!"

"Are we all invited to visit your king?" inquired Deborah. "I mean, does that include Joshua? I don't know if he can leave the coal mine?"

"Yes! You are all expected by the King," insisted Captain Mudd, with some irritation. "We know that Joshua is a spirit. He can come to the magical lands of the Nome Kingdom and Oz, if he is invited."

"As for you, Joshua," continued Captain Mudd, "of all the humans I've met, you are the only one I think I can like. All the other humans always looked so ugly to us nomes. You're different."

"But his clothes are all falling apart, and so is he," exclaimed Tommy. "And he doesn't have any color in his skin."

"And his looks are so ghostly and scary," continued Katie. "It takes time for one to just be willing to look at him."

"You know that Joshua is dead?" added Deborah.

"As I said," restated Captain Mudd, "he is my favorite human, and I really like the fact that he doesn't smile much! Now you will follow me down to the shore line and then to the tunnel. You will find a cart waiting to carry all of you to the Nome King."

"How did you get here?" asked Deborah. "As far as we can find out, there is no way to get out of here."

"We are Nomes!" answered Captain Mudd. "We are the fairies of the underground. Anywhere there are minerals, we nomes can go!"

"I thought you specialized in precious minerals!" remarked Tommy.

"Well, we do!" agreed Captain Mudd. "All the gold, silver, and precious stones we find are taken to our King. But we do know where to find other minerals, such as coal and oil."

"Then you know about this coal mine?" asked Katie.

"Yes, we do!" replied Captain Mudd. "And since it is a LOST MINE, it now belongs to the Nome King. So you are trespassing!"

"But this is Eastern Kentucky!" complained Deborah. "This isn't the magic Nome Kingdom! If it was, then Sigi could talk like a human. Sig say a few words."

Sigi growled at the Nomes, and Rocky hissed at them.

"Is that the best you can do for talking, Sigi?" asked Tommy.

To this Sigi replied with an, "Arf! Arf!"

"As you just heard," announced Deborah, "we are not in the magic Nome Kingdom! However, we are still glad to see you! And we don't want to keep the Nome King waiting."

"Speak for yourself," said Tommy. "I could use some breakfast before we go visiting."

"So could I," added Katie.

"I don't suppose you brought anything to eat with you, Captain Mudd?" asked Deborah. "Our selection of food is limited."

Captain Mudd replied, "The King did send a basket of food for you, although I can't imagine why he would care about you trespassers being hungry." With that, Captain Mudd had two nomes bring forth a picnic basket full of things for breakfast.

So the trespassers ate a hearty breakfast. There were things in the basket that each person liked. Sigi and Rocky also had special treats to eat. The only normal breakfast food missing was eggs, since nomes fear eggs. Everyone ate their fill.

When they had finished eating, they got ready to leave.

Deborah said, "We are ready to go see the Nome King."

"Are we prisoners?" asked Tommy.

"Where are the handcuffs and chains?" inquired Katie.

"Well, you're really to be guests of the Nome King!" responded Captain Mudd. "You are not prisoners! Would you be so kind as to follow me?"

With that, Captain Mudd led the way down the lake shore about one hundred feet. Here they found a freshly made tunnel. They entered the tunnel and found two motorized carts waiting for them. Deborah, Katie, Tommy, Rocky, and Sigi got in the front cart along with Captain Mudd and a driver. The rest of the nomes got into the second cart.

They were soon traveling along the tunnel with amazing speed. At this rate, it only took a few minutes to travel to the Nome Kingdom. Along the way they noticed that there were many tunnels leading off this tunnel.

"We are here! If you will just follow me through this side tunnel, we will be in the main cave of the Nome Kingdom," requested Captain Mudd.

So, everyone got out of the carts and followed Captain Mudd. They found themselves standing in the great cave of the Nome Kingdom. This was where the Nome King reviewed his vast army.

"We just need to travel a short distance along this side of the cave," stated Captain Mudd, "that will get us to the entrance to the throne room."

Everyone just followed Captain Mudd. The many nomes in the cave paid no attention to the visitors. Shortly, they were led through another short tunnel to the throne room. Here the Steward announced their arrival.

"Your Majesty!" said the Steward. "it is my disgusting duty to announce the arrival of those meddling humans and their disgusting pets, led by a relative of that do-gooder, Princess Dorothy of Oz"

"Humans, this is King Kaliko of the Nomes," finished the Steward.

"Be gone with you, Steward," replied the King. "If you can't give me good news then don't bother me."

"Well, its nice to meet you too, King Kaliko," greeted Deborah, who was trying to remember what she knew about nomes and their bad matters from reading books about the Land of Oz. "I see you still have your good disposition! I hope everything is going well in the Nome Kingdom?"

"Yes! Everything is going well," replied a grumpy King Kaliko. "I am glad to see that Captain Mudd was able to find you. It seems Ozma of Oz and your relative Dorothy, are worried about you."

"I should have guessed we had some help with our problem," stated Deborah. "Are they the reason for our visit here?"

"I thought we were prisoners," remarked Tommy and Katie together.

"Yes! Ozma and Dorothy asked us to find you," answered King Kaliko. "And no, you are not prisoners. You are my guests. You will be shown quarters where you can freshen up and rest. Afterwards I would like to have you join me for lunch."

"That is, except for those dogs of yours!" continued the King. "You know how I hate dogs!"

"I am not a dog!" replied Rocky, much to his own surprise at being able to speak.

"Now I know that we are in the Magic Nome Kingdom," remarked Deborah. "The animals can talk!"

The King ignored Deborah. However, he took another look at Rocky.

"Well I'll be!" observed King Kaliko. "If you aren't the nicest dog, I've ever seen. I especially like the mask over your eyes and the striped tail. I believe you would make a good hat!"

Rocky exploded, "What? That's how you treat your guests? You make them into hats?"

"Not really!" said Deborah. "He just gave you a compliment. You need to get used to the manner of nomes."

"I think I like you, Rocky!" announced King Kaliko. "Your manners are almost as bad as mine. I'll tell you what I'll do. Just to show you that there are no hard feelings, I am inviting the dogs to lunch as well as the humans."

"I am not a dog," protested Rocky again.

"I am the King and you are in my kingdom," responded Kaliko. "If I say you are a dog, then you are a dog. What do you have to say to that, Rocky?"

"Arf! Arf!" replied Rocky.

"Well, now that we are all friends again," said the King. "My servants will take you to your quarters."

So Deborah, Katie, Tommy, Rocky, and Sigi were led away to the plain but comfortable guest quarters. They met the needs of all the humans and animals very well. The humans were able to wash up and get new clothes to wear. Meanwhile, their old clothes were sent out, hopefully to get cleaned. The animals were groomed and fed. Everyone then got some rest. Deborah left orders for the servants to wake them about eleven-thirty.

At eleven-thirty, Deborah, Katie, and Tommy got up and dressed for lunch. Joshua had no need to change, since he only had the one image as a ghost. The "dogs" were groomed and ready.

Chapter 10
Lunch with the
Nome King

The servants came for Deborah and the others at noon.

"Hurry!" commanded the head servant. "You mustn't keep the King waiting. Lunch is ready."

"And what happens if we do keep him waiting?" asked Tommy.

"Oh! You don't want to do that," cried a servant. "If you did, the King would have us sliced and fed to the Seven-Headed Dog!"

"Well, we wouldn't want that to happen," agreed Katie. "We better hurry."

"We seem to be all ready," remarked Deborah, "so just lead the way and we will follow you."

The servants led the way to the Kings Dining Room. Deborah went first, then Katie, Tommy, Joshua, Rocky, and Sigi. They were ushered into the King's presence.

The Steward said in a loud voice, "Announcing the arrival of the pesky human, Deborah, and her party of do-gooders."

"Well, I am glad to see that you could make it!" responded King Kaliko. "As you can see, there are place markers for each of you. Please take you places."

"Why that's very kind of you Your Majesty," replied Deborah.

Everyone took his/her place at the round table. Joshua was seated on one side of the King with Deborah on the other side. Next to Deborah, sat Katie and then came Tommy. Sigi was next to Tommy.

Captain Mudd was next to Tommy. Finally, Rocky was seated between Captain Mudd and Joshua.

There were many different kinds of food dishes on the table. These included mushrooms of all varieties. There were truffles, roots, and herbs of many types. Fruits from the trees in the metal forest were present. Some human foods were also included. But of course, there were no egg dishes, for nomes are afraid of eggs; since if they touch one they loss their immortality.

"Well now, Rocky!" began the Nome King. "How did you come to be a pet of one of these humans?"

"I am not a pet, Your Majesty!" stated Rocky. "Actually, I got tangled up with these humans when I tried to get away from them at the graveyard. They chased me until I ran out of places to hide in. I only joined up with them because they offered me some food."

"If you don't like humans, then I think I like you even better than before," remarked the King. "If you ever need a new home, just let me know!"

"Now then, Joshua!" said the King. "I understand that you are a dead human?"

"Yes Your Majesty," answered Joshua. "I died about two-hundred years ago."

"So do all dead humans look like you?" continued the King as he still ignored the others in Deborah's party.

"Well, no Your Majesty," replied Joshua. "I am just a ghost. Most humans pass on to their eternal reward after death and don't become ghosts."

"Those are nice decorations you are wearing on your head and back," commented King Kaliko.

"Those are what killed me, Your Majesty," responded Joshua. "The knife in my back and the hatchet in my head were placed there by my ex-partners in the lost mine."

"So you mean all humans are not do-gooders like Deborah and her friends?" continued the King.

"Oh! By the way," announced the King. "The rest of you may start to eat. If you can't reach something, just ask the servant behind you to get it for you."

"No Your Majesty," replied Joshua. "Some humans are out just to become rich."

"Tell me, Joshua," continued the King. "What do you think about meeting the Nomes?"

"Well, I never knew that Nomes existed before," stated Joshua. "Is it true that you are responsible for all the valuable minerals in the world?"

"We nomes are responsible for much of the valuable minerals in the earth!" remarked King Kaliko. "We are underground fairies. The minerals near the surface of the earth belong to the humans."

"But when we were captured by the nomes," recalled Joshua, "Captain Mudd said that since the coal mine we were in was a lost mine, that it belonged to you. Therefore, we were trespassers and prisoners."

"Did you really say that, Captain Mudd?" asked the Nome King.

"Well, yes Your Majesty," replied Captain Mudd. "The humans didn't seem too pleased to see us nomes. I thought it would make it easier to get them to come here."

"I like the idea of all lost mines belonging to me!" announced King Kaliko. "That was very clever of you, Captain Mudd. For your service of claiming that mine for me, I am going to make you a Major!"

"Major Mudd does seem to be one of your more loyal nomes," added Tommy. "But I wish he would get a haircut!"

"Get a haircut!" laughed the King. "Now that's a good joke. I will have to remember that. I do suppose that you humans find us nomes a little on the hairy side."

"A little on the hairy side doesn't begin to cover it, Your Majesty," remarked Katie.

"I must assume that Your Majesty finds us humans a little on the bald side," stated Deborah. "And even if Major Mudd did bring us here as trespassers, Your Majesty, we are most grateful for your rescuing us from that mine."

"Yes!" laughed the King. "I do believe you got yourselves in a jam this time. If Ozma hadn't contacted us, I do believe you would still be trapped in that mine. What a fine end that would have been for a relative of Princess Dorothy of Oz!"

"I am sure this is all working toward some purpose," added Deborah, as she ignored the Kings last remark.

"Well, yes, it must," agreed the King. "As soon as we finish having this lunch, I have been requested to send you on your way to visit Ozma. No doubt she will want to punish you for your behavior."

"No doubt she will want to see us in relationship to our recent behavior," agreed Deborah.

"No doubt!" repeated the King. "Ozma gave us permission to reopen the Nome Tunnel as far as Winkie Country. Major Mudd will accompany you through the tunnel under the deadly desert to Winkie Country. From there, you will be furnished transportation by Ozma."

"So, Ozma knows we are coming?" asked Tommy.

"Why yes!" replied the King. "As soon as I was informed about your safe rescue from the mine, I had a message send to Ozma. She is waiting for you in the Emerald City."

"But I see that you have finished eating," announced The King. "So I think it is time that you all were on your way to visit Ozma."

"I want to thank Your Majesty for the honor of having lunch with you," announced Deborah. "But we have taken up far too much of your time. May we not meet again for a long time!"

"Now that's an exit line I will have to remember," laughed the King. "Major Mudd, if you would be so kind as to get these humans and their pets out of my sight."

"Yes Your Majesty" responded Major Mudd. "At once Your Majesty. What's everyone waiting for? Let's go!"

So Deborah and her party got up from the table and followed Major Mudd out into the hallway tunnel. He led them back to the great cave. Here a motorized cart was waiting to take them to Oz.

Once everyone had gotten into the cart, Major Mudd had the driver head for the Nome Tunnel that led to the Land of Oz. Within a few minutes, the cart entered the tunnel. There was nothing to see on this trip but the walls of the tunnel. The trip under the deadly desert only took a few minutes. Finally, they emerged from the tunnel into daylight in the Land of Oz.

Chapter 11
The Trip to the
Emerald City

They were now in Winkie Country of the Land of Oz. Since Deborah, Katie, Tommy, Rocky, and Sigi had not seen daylight for what seemed like several days they found the sight very pleasing.

"Wow!" exclaimed Katie, with a broad smile. "For a while there I thought that I might never see the sun again."

"Yes!" agreed Tommy. "It is nice to be back out of the earth."

"Even if the grass and trees have a yellow color," stated Deborah, "it is nice to be in the sunlight again. I wonder where we are and who that is waiting for us?"

"This is the Winkie Country of the Land of Oz," announced Major Mudd. "That is Dorothy Gail, the Wizard of Oz, and the Wooden Sawhorse of Oz waiting for you. They will take you to see Ozma of Oz."

"Thank you, Major Mudd, for rescuing us and for transporting us to Oz," replied Deborah, as she and the others got out of the nome cart.

"Yes, thank you," added Katie and Tommy together.

"I was only doing my duty," responded Major Mudd. "You don't owe me anything for it. Besides, if it wasn't for that rescue, I wouldn't have gotten to meet Joshua. I never knew humans could look so good."

"Well, for a nome, you're not that bad," added Joshua. "And since you, Major Mudd, were the first nome I have met, I will try to think of all nomes being like you."

Everyone finished saying goodbye to Major Mudd. Major Mudd then had the driver take the cart back into the Nome Tunnel and headed back to the Nome Kingdom.

"Auntie," asked Katie, "now that Joshua has been helpful to us, what are we going to do about his problem? I mean, Joshua did everything he could to help us. Isn't there some way to help him?"

"Yes, Auntie," pleaded Tommy, "Joshua has helped us and taught us about ghosts and not to be afraid of them. He helped us to catch the fish and explored things for us. Surely we can do something for him?"

"Well, you two are right," agreed Deborah. "Joshua did uphold his part of the bargain. Now, we need to see what we can do for him. I have a feeling that this visit to Ozma of Oz might help us with Joshua's problem."

Deborah and the others went over to the carriage where Dorothy, the Sawhorse, and the Wizard were waiting for them.

"Hi! Sawhorse," remarked Katie. "You look like you are just a wooden horse. Why are you hitched to the front of that carriage?"

"Why I am going to pull the carriage to the Emerald City," said the Sawhorse, as he turned toward Katie.

"Wow!" exclaimed Tommy. "Now we have a talking wooden sawhorse that moves and can pull carriages. This is even more difficult to believe than believing in ghosts!"

"We have a murder to solve!" stated Deborah. "Come on let's meet our relative, Dorothy Gail of Kansas."

They climbed into the carriage.

"Hello, Dorothy Gail and Wizard!" greeted Deborah. "Dorothy, I understand that we are related. And this is my niece, Katie, and nephew, Tommy. Here we have Joshua Smith, Sigi my dog, and Rocky a raccoon."

"Hello, Deborah, Katie, Tommy, Joshua, Sigi, and Rocky; I am Dorothy Gail, one of Deborah's ancestor that disappeared around 1900 from Kansas," replied Dorothy. "I am now a Princess of Oz."

"But that would mean you are one hundred years old," remarked Tommy.

"And you don't look a day older than nine years old," cried Katie.

"I am only nine years old since that is the age I was when I moved to the Land of Oz," explained Dorothy. "I can't grow older while I am in Oz."

"You mean the stories we have heard about the Land of Oz are true?" asked Deborah.

"Yes! The stories you have heard about the Land of Oz are true," announced Dorothy. "I was seeing how all my relatives in the outside world were doing, using Ozma's Magic Picture, when I discovered you were trapped in the mine. I asked Ozma to help you out."

"So, this is your new friend, Joshua," requested Dorothy.

"Yes!" replied Deborah. "Joshua Smith, this is Dorothy Gail. Dorothy, this is the late Joshua Smith. He is a ghost!"

"Wow!" exclaimed a thrilled Dorothy. "I don't get to meet many ghosts. I must say you don't look very well!"

"It is a pleasure to meet you, Dorothy," responded Joshua. "I am afraid that I haven't been myself for about two-hundred years."

"It does look like you died unexpectedly," agreed Dorothy.

"The knife in my back and the hatchet in my head ended my life," continued Joshua. "I was murdered, but since my killers were never discovered, I must wander the murder site forever!"

"Do I understand correctly that if we can find and punish your murderers, then you can go to the after life?" asked Dorothy.

"That's about it," answered Joshua. "But it's been too long! How can you punish my dead murderer?"

"First let us establish the facts about your death," suggested Dorothy. "After that is done, we will see what can be done for you!"

"Perhaps Ozma's Enchanted Picture can show us what happened?" suggested the Wizard. "That is, if it can see into the past!"

"I think it is worth a try," agreed Dorothy. "Before we can do that we need to go the Emerald City where Ozma's Enchanted Picture is located. So Sawhorse, will you take us to the Emerald City by way of Gillikin Country?"

"As you command, Dorothy," replied the Sawhorse.

"And please go slow enough so that Deborah, Katie, Tommy, and Joshua can see some of the sights!" continued Dorothy. "After two-hundred years, an hour or two won't make any difference."

"It is your time to waste as you please," responded the Sawhorse. He started moving at what he considered to be a slow pace.

"Do you think I could have a closer look at the knife and hatchet, Joshua?" requested the Wizard.

"Well, I guess so," agreed Joshua. "Why do you want to see them?"

"If we are lucky," stated the Wizard, "maybe there will be something on them that will identify their owner."

So Joshua brought his back close to the Wizard. The Wizard then looked very closely at the handle of the knife.

"I am not sure," said the Wizard, "but I think there may be initials craved in the handle of the knife. Joshua, can you sharpen up your image a little?"

"I'll try!" replied Joshua. He then brought his image into its sharpest focus.

"That's better!" remarked the Wizard. "I definitely see the initials of W. F. Deborah, can you see if you see the initials as well?"

Joshua moved over to Deborah and turned his back toward her. Deborah looked at the knife handle.

"I believe I do see the initials W. F." agreed Deborah. "But Joshua Smith would have initials of J. S. So I wonder whose initials are these."

"How does Walter Flounder sound?" suggested Joshua. "He was one of my ex-business partners in the mine."

"Didn't we see his grave in the lost graveyard?" asked Tommy.

"I am sure that was one of the names we found," added Katie.

"So, that does make it look like Joshua was murdered," announced Dorothy. "Are there any other clues that you can see, Wizard?"

"I haven't looked at the hatchet yet," responded the Wizard. "Perhaps there are some more interesting marks on it? Joshua, can I have a look at the hatchet?"

"Sure thing," answered Joshua. So, Joshua moved back over to the Wizard and held the hatchet at his eye level.

The Wizard looked over the left side of the handle without finding any marks. Next he looked at the end of the handle. Still, there were no marks. Finally he asked Joshua to turn his head so he could look at the right side of the handle. Still, there was nothing to be seen.

"Well, the handle doesn't have any marks on it," replied the Wizard. "Does anyone have any ideas on where to look next?"

"Try looking at the axe head where it connects to the handle," suggested Joshua. "Some people had their hatchets engraved when they gave them to someone."

"I'll try that," agreed the Wizard. He looked at the right side of the axe head and found nothing. Next he looked at the left side of the axe head. Finally he found something.

"Well, I'll be," exclaimed the Wizard. "It says given to Benjamin Black by Joshua Smith!"

"And that was my other ex-business partner!" exclaimed Joshua. "I guess one needs to be very careful in choosing business partners. I thought we were all friends and would split the profits from the mine three ways."

"It looks like the only thing they tried to split three ways was you, Joshua!" remarked Tommy.

"Joshua was really murdered!" stated an excited Katie. "Wow! I've never met a murdered person before. I am sure not many people have ever gotten to talk to a murdered person."

While everyone had been paying attention to Joshua, the trees and grass had changed from a yellow hue to a purple hue. The carriage had crossed from Winkie Country into Gillikin Country.

"Oh my!" said Tommy. "I've never seen purple grass and trees before."

"That's right," agreed Dorothy. "You don't know about the different colors for different sections of the Land of Oz."

"And the houses are purple and people wear purple clothes," exclaimed Katie.

"You could say that the favorite color in Gillikin Country is purple," added Dorothy. "By the way Wizard, where are we?"

"I haven't been paying much attention to the scenery," replied the Wizard. "Perhaps if the Sawhorse would slow down a bit, I could read a road sign."

"Slow, slow, and slower," complained the Sawhorse, "all you want to do is waste time. All right, I'm slowing down!"

"I think I see a crossroad coming up," announced Tommy.

"Yes, you do," Katie agreed, "and there is a sign post there."

"Sawhorse!" requested the Wizard. "Would you mind stopping at that road sign?"

"Well, if we really must know where we are," answered the Sawhorse, "I suppose I can stop there."

The Sawhorse stopped the carriage at the sign post.

Deborah read the sign post. It said Chessville was to the right at a distance of one-half mile. On the left was Checkerville a distance of one-fourth mile.

"Dorothy! Do we have we time to visit one of these villages?" asked Tommy.

"Yes, Dorothy!" pleaded Katie. "We would like to see some of Oz."

"Well, I think we can spare some time," replied Dorothy. "Which way shall we turn?"

Chapter 12
A Visit to Chessville

"I think I would like to see why a town would be called Chessville," stated a curious Tommy. "I vote for turning right!"

"Just because you play chess and I only play checkers," complained Katie, "is no reason to overlook a town called Checkerville. I vote we turn left."

"Actually, both names seem strange to me," remarked Joshua. "Can't we visit both towns?"

"I think we should visit both towns, too," added Dorothy. "I don't think I have ever been to either of them before."

"Sawhorse," called the Wizard. "Would you kindly take us to Chessville?"

"As you wish," replied the Sawhorse and pulled the carriage down the road on the right. It was only a matter of a few minutes before the Sawhorse stopped in the middle of Chessville. There were no houses in sight; however, there were two buildings that looked like barns, on opposite sides of a giant chess board in front of the carriage. The barn on the right was painted white. The barn on the left was painted black. Each barn had sixteen stalls.

After a few moments, giant chess pieces started coming from the barns and gathering around the giant chess board.

"Good day to you folks!" greeted the White King. "Who do we have here? Which of you is going to command the White Pieces? Come now! Don't be shy."

"The chess pieces walk and talk!" exclaimed an amazed Katie.

"Can I play the White Pieces?" requested Tommy.

"I guess we can stay a few minutes," stated Dorothy. "Sure, Tommy, you can play the White Pieces."

"And who will command the Black Pieces?" demanded the Black King. "I doubt that it will take much to beat this boy."

"Don't look at me!" exclaimed Joshua. "I've never heard of chess."

"Well, I don't know much about chess," replied Katie. "Would you like to play the Black Pieces, Auntie?"

"I don't know much about chess, either!" answered Deborah. "How about Katie and I play against Tommy? Would that be all right with you, Tommy?"

"That's fine with me," agreed Tommy. "Remember that this is just a friendly game of chess. Okay?"

"Okay!" replied everyone.

So Tommy sat in a tall chair on the white side of the chess board. Katie and Deborah sat in the tall chair on the black side of the chess board. The White and Black Kings had their pieces take their places on the chess board. Everything was ready for the game to begin.

"What do we do now, Katie?" requested Deborah.

"We wait for Tommy to make the first move," stated Katie. "White moves first in the game of chess."

"Okay, Tommy," called Katie. "It's your move!"

"All right," shouted Tommy back to Katie, "I want the King's Pawn to move forward two squares to the King's four square."

"An excellent move!" commented the White King. "Move forward two squares, King's Pawn!"

With that, the King's Pawn moved forward two squares.

"Don't let him worry you," remarked the Black King. "That was a very old fashioned move for which we have many good responses!"

"What do you suggest, Katie?" asked Deborah.

"The simplest reply is to move the King's Pawn to the King's four square," replied Katie. "Unless you have a better move, then I suggest just making that reply."

"That sounds good to me," said Deborah. "So, will the King's Pawn move to the King's four square!"

"That move is okay," stated the Black King, "but it is a little old fashioned. Why not give the boy some trouble by playing Queen's Bishop Pawn to Queen's Bishop four?"

"I don't know that move, Auntie?" remarked Katie. "Do you think it's fair to have the Black King helping us?"

"It's only a game for fun!" Deborah reminded her. "Let's see if the Black King knows what he is doing."

"Okay, Auntie," agreed Katie, "but you have me at a loss on how to continue the game!"

"Queen's Bishop Pawn!" commanded the Black King. "Forward two squares."

The Queen's Bishop Pawn moved forward two squares.

"Careful!" cautioned the White King to Tommy. "They are trying to get tricky. They want you to move your Queen's Pawn out so they can trade it for their Queen's Bishop Pawn."

"But why would they want to do that?" asked Tommy.

"Why so they would have two Pawns in the center of the board to our one Pawn!" responded the White King. "Surely, you know how important it is to control the center of the board in a game of chess?"

"Of course, I know that," replied Tommy, even though he didn't know it. "Perhaps it would be better if I let you help me with this game, Your Majesty?"

"Well, if you think that is best," replied the White King. "I would be only too happy to help you."

So the White King took charge of the White pieces.

"Knight to King's Bishop three," called the White King. And the White King Knight moved to the King's Bishop three square.

"Let's see if we can put pressure on their King's Pawn," suggested the Black King, without even asking Deborah and Katie what they wanted to do.

"Pawn to King's Knight three!" command the Black King. The King's Knight Pawn moved forward one square.

"Now we have a game going!" shouted the White King. "Pawn to Queen's four."

"I thought I was commanding the White Pieces," stated Tommy.

"But, of course you are!" replied the White King. "However, you do want to make a game of it, don't you?"

"I'll take your advice," agreed Tommy, but his heart wasn't in it.

"Now's our chance," announced the Black King. "Pawn takes Pawn!"

With that, the Black and White Pawns staged a short battle. Finally, the White Pawn fell down and played dead. The White Pawn was carried from the game board and the Black Pawn took over its square.

"Wait a moment," called a confused Deborah, "I thought that Katie and I were in charge here?"

"But of course you are," replied the Black King. "Surely you can see that we now have the White Pieces just where we want them."

"Frankly, I think the game is still very even, or at least it will be when Tommy takes back the Pawn with his Knight!" remarked Katie.

"It is okay, Katie," Deborah assured her. "Let's just watch how the chess pieces play the game."

The game then began to speed up, for the two Kings had played this same game many times before. As Katie had predicated, Tommy's Knight took the Black Pawn.

Finally, the pieces began to fly across the board faster and faster. Deborah, Katie, and Tommy were no longer able to keep track of the game. So, they quietly climbed down from the tall chairs and walked back toward the carriage. None of the pieces seemed to notice their leaving the game.

Shortly thereafter the game ended in a draw. Afterwards, both sets of pieces came back on the board to congratulate their respective Kings.

"Good game, Your Majesty," called all the pieces to their respective kings.

"But the game would have been even better if you hadn't traded me for a Bishop," remarked one of Knights. "Everyone knows a Knight is better than a Bishop. After all, I can attack another type of piece without being under attack in return!"

"But I can move further in one move than a Knight!" boasted a Bishop.

"Possibly," commented a Rook, "but you can only travel on half of the board!"

"Enough!" shouted the White Queen. "I have as many choices of direction as a Knight, and I can move much further in a single move; therefore, I am the most powerful and important piece on the board."

"You are all wrong," cried a Pawn, much to the disgust of the other pieces. "I can be promoted to any other piece except a King. So, I become whichever one is needed most at that time. Therefore, I am the most powerful and important piece!"

"That will do!" commanded a King. "I may move slowly, but if you lose me, the game is over! Now who do you think is most important to the game?"

"Well," murmured all the pieces. "We guess the King is most important!"

"Fine!" stated the other King. "Now let's all line up for another game."

"I think we should be leave," suggested Deborah.

"We're with you," responded Katie and Tommy.

Deborah and the others ran to the carriage and quickly got aboard.

"Sawhorse," requested the Wizard, "kindly get us out of here."

"Very well," replied the Sawhorse. He then turned the carriage around and made a run for the main road. When he reached the main road, he stopped.

The Sawhorse asked, "Which way now?"

"Let's try for Checkerville," replied Dorothy. "But go slowly."

"Okay!" responded Sawhorse, as he started off to Checkerville at a slow pace.

"Dorothy," asked Deborah, "where did the citizens of Chessville come from?"

"We used to have a giant chessboard at the palace," stated Dorothy. "It used life-sized pieces. It took a couple of men to move the larger pieces about the board during a game. Someone came up with the idea of bringing the chess pieces to life so they could move themselves. Unfortunately, giving the pieces life made them want to do more than just move about a chessboard at some other person's command."

"Let me guess. The pieces want to tell others how to play the game," said Katie. "They also seem to argue over which of them is better."

"True! Each type of piece thinks it is better than the other types," added Tommy. "They emphasize their differences rather than the fact that they are all needed for a game of chess."

"Yes, they act almost like humans," remarked the Wizard.

Chapter 13
A Visit to Checkerville

"Well, I hope the citizens of Checkerville are different from those of Chessville," remarked Deborah.

"Of course they will be,," stated Katie.

"After all," commented Tommy, "all the checker pieces are alike!"

Shortly the Sawhorse stopped the carriage before a large playing board. On opposite sides of the board were two large boxes with doors in them.

"Oh, no," announced Tommy, "not another chessboard."

"It's not a chessboard," stated Katie. "It's a checkerboard. Don't you see the numbers from 1 to 32 on the Black squares? Square 32 is on the Red players lower right. The game of checkers only uses the 32 dark colored squares."

"Well, so far, this looks very similar to Chessville!" commented Deborah.

"Definitely not!" replied a voice from one of the boxes. "You couldn't be further from the truth. We citizens of Checkerville could never be as stuck up as those citizens of Chessville!"

"Right!" agreed a piece from the box on the other side of the board. "The Chessville citizens are always fighting over what type of piece is most important. Here in Checkerville we are all of the same type, and thus are equal!"

"Now, they do sound nicer," admitted Tommy. "Perhaps we could get down and visit for a few minutes?"

"I think you should visit these citizens!" recommended Dorothy. "And you couldn't ask for a bigger game of checkers than this one. Do Katie and Tommy know how to play checkers?"

"Well, Tommy and I used to play checkers," recalled Katie, "but since Tommy learned chess, he doesn't play much checkers."

"Oh, I still think I can beat you at checkers!" boasted Tommy. "Come on, let's have a game."

So Deborah, Katie, and Tommy got down from the carriage and walked over to the large checkerboard.

"Would you like to play a game of checkers?" invited a Black Checker as he came out of the box on the right. "I assure you it will be a friendly game."

"I do know more about checkers than I do about chess," answered Katie. "If Tommy would consider playing the Red Checkers, he can have a game with me"

"I am not that good at checkers," stated Tommy, "but I will try to give you a good game. Maybe this time, Auntie can assist me?"

"Sure," agreed Deborah, "I'll help Tommy play the Red Pieces."

"That's a good idea! Auntie and I will take the Red Pieces," said Tommy.

"Then I will play the Black Pieces," announced Katie.

So Deborah and Tommy went to the right side of the board and Katie went to the left side of the board. Next, twelve pieces came out of each box and took their places on the board.

"Okay, Tommy! Whose turn is it?" asked Deborah.

"In checkers, Auntie, Black moves first!" remarked Katie.

"But in chess, White moves first," responded Deborah.

"What can we say?" remarked one of the Black pieces. "The citizens of Chessville just have everything backwards!"

"I see!" commented Deborah. "In that case, Katie, it's your move!"

"Let's move from square number eleven to square number fifteen," requested Katie. "It is the absolute best first move in checkers!"

"That's very good," stated the Checker on square eleven. It then moved to square fifteen.

"Well, Tommy, what move would you suggest we start with?" requested Deborah.

"The standard reply to this move is moving the piece on square twenty-three to square nineteen!" suggested Tommy. "So, let's make that move!"

"That can best be described as a Bookish move," remarked the Red Piece on square twenty-three. "Oh well, at least it is a good move. You could have made a weaker move such as square twenty-four to square twenty!"

So the Red Checker moved from square twenty-three to square nineteen.

"Oh dear!" exclaimed Deborah. "It looks like these Checkers have their own idea about how the game should be played."

"But of course we do!" responded several Checkers together. "After all, who should know more about playing checkers than the Checkers?"

"They have a good point," agreed Tommy. "Why don't we just let them demonstrate how to play checkers?"

"That sounds like a great idea!" said Deborah. "Katie, is it all right with you if we let the Checkers show us the finer points of the Game?"

"I think that's a fine idea," remarked Katie. "Why didn't I think of that?"

"Perhaps we should have them tell a little about why they are making each move?" suggested Tommy. "That is if the Checkers don't mind giving away some of their secrets?"

"We would be only too happy to demonstrate and tell you about the game of checkers," responded the group of Checkers.

So the Checkers proceeded with the game. As each Checker moved, it gave the reasons for the move. The game went quickly and ended in a draw.

"It would appear that if both sides play the game well," stated Tommy, "then the game should end in a draw. So both sides start out equally matched and each piece is of equal value!"

"Well, I would not go that far," announced the Checker which started on square eleven. "It is obvious that the Checkers on squares nine, ten, eleven and twelve are the most important. After all, these are the Checkers that must get the game started!"

"Now hold on a moment," called Checker number one. "If it weren't for the Checkers on the back row, the opponent's checkers could become kings very easily. We try very hard to prevent that! And one cannot win without some kings!"

"I think it is getting late," stated Deborah as she edged her way toward the carriage. "Don't you think we really must be going, Katie and Tommy?"

"Oh yes!" exclaimed Katie.

"I didn't know it was so late!" added Tommy. "We really should be off."

With that, everyone made a break for the carriage. They quickly got aboard and had the Sawhorse pull them out of Checkerville.

"Let me guess," announced Tommy. "These Checkers were brought to life so that people wouldn't have to move the pieces about the checker board."

"However, now they think they are the experts on the game!" remarked Katie.

"That's about the size of it," agreed Dorothy.

"So, why did you have us visit Chessville and Checkerville, Dorothy?" asked Deborah.

"So, you could see why one shouldn't play with the nature of things!" responded Dorothy. "Every time one tries to improve upon nature, one is likely to create a monster. Perhaps these examples will help you appreciate things the way they were meant to be?"

"Man gets lazy and brings things to life so he doesn't have to move them," stated Deborah. "Afterwards, he finds out that the things wish to live their own life!"

"Indeed! The checkers, who are all identical, still found some small differences to use to argue about who is best," remarked the Wizard. "Isn't that just like humans?"

"I think these citizens were very interesting!" explained Katie. "However, I see why you have to give them their own towns."

"All in all," commented Tommy, "it did make for an interesting visit."

"So Joshua, what do you think of the Land of Oz?" asked Deborah.

"Well it certainly isn't like anything I have ever seen before," replied Joshua. "Are there any normal people here in Oz?"

"Remember that this is a fairyland," stated Dorothy. "But there are at least beings that look and behave much more like you are used to. When we get to the Emerald City, I think you will find things a little more normal."

"I think we can go on to the Emerald City without any more stops," announced the Wizard. "Sawhorse, you may travel at a good safe speed. I think we have seen enough of the scenery!"

"Now that's more like it!" cried the Sawhorse. "Hold on tight! And away we go!"

Fortunately, everyone took the Sawhorses advice and got a good grip on the armrests and each other, for the Sawhorse was off in a flash. He started out so fast that poor Joshua was left floating behind the carriage.

"Hey, Joshua," called Tommy. "You better hurry up or we will lose you!"

"I am coming," shouted Joshua as he started out in hot pursuit. The carriage, being pulled by the Sawhorse, was moving faster than any thing Joshua had seen before. But being a ghost and not controlled by physical things, Joshua was soon able to catch up.

The party traveled along very quickly for over an hour. Just at sunset the carriage approached the Emerald City.

This was Joshua's first view of the Emerald City, and the city's green lights added to its splendor.

"Wow!" exclaimed Joshua. "That is a beautiful city. I don't think I have ever seen anything like it before."

"Slow down, Sawhorse," instructed Dorothy. "We will need to stop at the entrance."

So the Sawhorse slowed down.

Chapter 14
The Emerald City

The Sawhorse stopped the carriage at the entrance to the Emerald City. The Gate Guardian bowed to Princess Dorothy and opened the gate. He was waving the carriage through the gate when he first noticed Joshua.

"Your Highness!" warned the Guardian. "There's a ghost riding with you in the carriage. And it doesn't look very friendly!"

"Just how friendly would you look after you've been dead for two hundred years?" asked Joshua, as he floated out the carriage and moved toward the Guardian.

"But-t, bu-ut-tt, bu-ut-tt!" stuttered the Guardian.

"Behave Joshua!" scolded Deborah. "It is not nice to scare people, especially nice happy people!"

"Oh, Okay!" agreed Joshua, reluctantly. "I don't seem to get to have much fun as a ghost." He floated back to the carriage.

"It is okay, Guardian," assured Dorothy. "The Ghosts name is Joshua and he is my guest!"

"As you wish," replied the Guardian, as he tried to recover his composure. "Any guest of yours is welcome here, even if he is a ghost!"

"Onto the palace, if you please, Sawhorse," directed Dorothy, "and do be careful not to run over anyone."

"I'll be very careful," promised the Sawhorse. He proceeded at a very slow speed for him.

Progress through the crowded streets of the Emerald City was very slow. Of course all the inhabitants wanted to see Princess Dorothy. Deborah, Katie, Tommy, and Sigi were also welcome. Seeing Rocky the raccoon was a special treat.

However, most of the trouble came from everyone wanted to have a good look at Joshua the ghost. The knife sticking out of his back and the hatchet in his head caused much talk for the people watching the carriage. In their eagerness to see Joshua better, they kept blocking the streets. The poor Sawhorse found himself going much slower than he had intended.

Joshua, on the other hand, was busy looking at the citizens and buildings of the Emerald City. Never before had he seen so many emeralds. Emeralds were used to decorate all the buildings of the Emerald City. Most of the people in the city dressed in emerald green outfits. Joshua was also surprised at all the brightly lit shops. He hoped to get a chance to look at some of the shops later.

"Now, this is very interesting," stated Joshua. "Look at all these shops, these buildings, these people. The Emerald City is well worth the visit to the Land of Oz. Every one seems so happy!"

"We try very hard to keep all of the citizens of Oz happy," remarked Dorothy. "After all, this is a fairyland and is supposed to be a happy place."

"This is a big crowd just to meet us!" said Tommy.

"Yes!" agreed Katie. "And I don't think that this attention is just for our benefit, Tommy. Everyone seems to be looking at Joshua and Rocky."

"Well, these people don't get to see a raccoon or a ghost that often," explained Dorothy. "Come to think of it you only met your first ghost a few days ago! I am glad to see that the people of Oz do not seem to be afraid of a ghost!"

After much time and with much care, the Sawhorse finally pulled the carriage onto the palace grounds and into the courtyard. Here, Ozma, the Ruler of Oz, was waiting to greet them.

"Welcome, everyone!" greeted Ozma. "And may I give a special welcome to Joshua and Rocky. Please let my servants make you comfortable. After that, we can have dinner and discuss your problems!"

The servants helped everyone down from the carriage.

Everyone was shown to their rooms. Here they freshened up and got ready for dinner. Sigi and Rocky had their coats groomed. Deborah, Katie, and Tommy got new outfits to wear.

But Joshua got the best treat of all. Glinda the Good dropped by and arranged for Joshua to have a body during his stay at the palace. It was a temporary arrangement. However, it gave Joshua a chance to try out a new suit of clothes and the privilege of eating food like a human. He looked like he did before he had died. There was no knife in his back or hatchet in his head.

After everyone had freshened up, they gathered in the hallway. The others complimented Joshua on his revived appearance. The servants took them to Ozma's private quarters. Glinda the Good greeted them at the door and explained that Ozma was busy elsewhere on affairs of state. Deborah and her friends were joined at the dinner by Dorothy and some of her old friends, Nick Chopper known as the Tin Woodman, and Jack Pumpkinhead. Everyone except the Tin Woodman and Jack enjoyed a fine meal with Glinda. Nick and Jack did not eat.

The food at the table was of many varieties. There were favorite things there for everyone who could eat food. Even Sigi and Rocky had their favorite treats. All who did eat managed to over eat just like one does at Thanksgiving dinners. They ate until they thought that they could not possibly eat another bite.

"Wow!" remarked Joshua. "I never thought I would get to taste food again! You can't imagine how I have missed eating the last two-hundred years! Just the smell of the food is a great treat. Thank you, Glinda the Good for the use of this body."

"I'm sure you are most welcome!" responded Glinda. "It seemed like such a little gift when we considered the help you gave Deborah and her friends. But, please bear in mind that the body is temporary and will only exist within the Land of Oz!"

"I understand that the body is temporary," agreed Joshua. "I still appreciate it greatly. Never before have I seen so much food, and such a great variety of things to eat."

"Yes! The food here in Oz is very good!" agreed Tommy.

"I also have to say this was a good meal," commented Katie.

Dorothy announced, "I believe you have some ideas on how to help Joshua, don't you, Glinda?"

"Yes! I do," responded Glinda. "Dorothy! After dinner, Ozma has given us her permission to use her Enchanted Picture. Hopefully, it will give us ideas on what to do next!"

"That's a good idea for starters!" agreed Dorothy. "If we can get a good picture of what actually happened to Joshua, then maybe we will get some hints on how best to help him. It is always nice to know the facts about a crime!"

"Well, I am willing to try anything to solve my problem," added Joshua. "I must also say what a privilege it is to meet the Tin Woodman and Jack Pumpkinhead. I never dreamed that a tin woodman or pumpkinhead stick man could be brought to life!"

"The Tin Woodman once had a flesh and blood body like other citizens of Oz," remarked Dorothy. "However, an old witch enchanted his axe so that it kept cutting off parts of him. Each time he chopped off a part, a tin smith made him a replacement part from tin. Finally he was all made out of tin, and that's how Nick Chopper became the Tin Woodman."

"Is that really true?" questioned Tommy, Katie, and Deborah together.

"Oh, yes!" responded the Tin Woodman. "However, she left out the part about my being in love with Nimmie Aimee, a young lady that lived with the witch."

"And we don't get to see a ghost often," stated Jack.

"We only wished we had seen you before you were lent the new body!" added the Tin Woodman.

"I am sure that I will be a ghost again before I leave Oz," said Joshua. "I will try to make sure you two get to see me then. Meanwhile, I think this visit to Oz more then makes up for what little help I was able to give Deborah's party."

"But the deal was that if you tried to help us," recalled Deborah, "then we would try to help you. We plan to do our best to keep that deal!"

"I greatly appreciate your help!" acknowledged Joshua. "No matter what the final outcome, I am glad to have met you."

"It has been very interesting meeting you too!" Katie assured him.

"You are our first ghost!" added Tommy.

'We must thank Her Majesty for this wonderful dinner, and for sending the Nomes to find us in that cave!" stated Deborah. "Things weren't looking very good to us back there. It is really a pleasure being here!"

"It is a pleasure to have you here," replied Glinda. "I will give Ozma your thanks. Now before we get to work on Joshua's problem, can I interest anyone in dessert?"

"Well, maybe I can eat a small dessert," remarked Tommy. "I am awfully full, but I'm willing to give it a try."

All the others decided that they too would try a little dessert, except for the Tin Woodman and Jack.

So, Glinda had the servants pass around a dessert tray. On the tray was every kind of dessert that Katie and Tommy had ever seen before. In addition, there were some new desserts, such as plum pudding, rice pudding, fruit tarts, and fruit cakes, which were previously unknown to Katie and Tommy. These were from Joshua's time.

Once dessert was over, the group gathered around Ozma's Enchanted Picture.

Chapter 15
The Enchanted Picture

The Enchanted Picture was on the far wall of Ozma's sitting room. At present, it looked just like any other picture on a wall.

"As Dorothy can tell you," exclaimed Glinda, "Ozma's Enchanted Picture can be used to see what everyone is doing right now. She used it earlier to locate Deborah, Katie, Tommy, and Sigi. It seems Dorothy wanted to see some of her present day relatives. That is how Ozma knew you were lost in the old coal mine!"

"Now what we want to do is see if it can show us what happened to Joshua, almost two hundred years ago!" continued Glinda. "I have never tried to use the Enchanted Picture to locate a dead person, or to see into the past. However, since Oz and the outside world do not exist in the same time line, it may just be possible!"

Deborah asked, "So how do we use this Enchanted Picture?"

"Well, I just tell it who and/or what I want to see," replied Glinda. "For example, Enchanted Picture, show us the funeral of Sarah Smith!"

At once the scene in the picture frame disappeared and the lost graveyard came into view. There were grave markers for Jackie Murphy Smith, Daniel Potts, and Joshua Smith. A new grave had been dug for Sarah Smith. There were six or seven persons gather around a coffin. It was a rainy day.

The sight of the funeral brought tears to Joshua's eyes.

"In all my problems," remarked Joshua, "I forgot all about my wife Sarah. What happened to her?"

"Sarah died of a broken heart two years after you disappeared," stated Deborah, "or at least that's what the grave marker says."

"Oh dear!" responded Joshua. "You mean she didn't even know that I was dead?"

"I am afraid not!" replied Glinda. "Your ex-partners covered up their crime well."

"As you can see, Deborah," continued Glinda. "It does appear that we can look at some past events! Now let's try for the event of Joshua's murder! Enchanted Picture, we want to see Joshua's murder!"

Everyone waited patiently while the scene changed once more. This time the Picture showed Joshua, Walter, and Benjamin. They were standing at the end of one of the tunnels in the mine, looking up at a coal seam. There was a bright yellow streak showing in the coal seam.

"We've done it" shouted Walter. "We've found gold!"

"Eureka!" cried Benjamin.

"I don't believe it!" exclaimed Joshua. "No one finds gold in a coal vein."

"Well, we did!" stated Walter and Benjamin. "We're rich!"

The three of them danced around for joy. It was during this rejoicing that somehow Walter and Benjamin slipped behind Joshua. The next thing Joshua felt was a sharp pain in his back where Walter had pushed in the knife. Before Joshua could scream, Benjamin struck him in the head with a hatchet. That was the end of Joshua's life.

"What do we do with the body, partner?" asked Walter.

"We stuff it in the first tunnel on the left, just like we planned!' replied Benjamin. "Everyone knows that there has been a cave-in in that tunnel. No one will notice that it is about to become five feet shorter."

So Benjamin and Walter carried Joshua's body back to the first tunnel on the left. There they placed Joshua's body up against the landslide and pulled down more rocks and dirt on top of him. When they were done, they simply went outside and had lunch like nothing had happened. They ate all the food that had been left for lunch for the three of them. They were even careful to use Joshua's dishes, so it looked like he had eaten lunch as well.

It wasn't until nightfall that anyone bothered asking about where was Joshua?

"Where's Joshua?" asked Sarah. "Have you two seen my husband?"

"Why no!" replied Benjamin. "I haven't seen him since lunch time."

"I think I remember him visiting his still after lunch," remarked Walter, "afterwards, he went back into the mine. I haven't seen him since then."

"Thank you, Enchanted Picture," called Glinda, and the Enchanted Picture returned to its original picture.

"It does seem that Joshua was murdered," stated Katie.

"Yes," agreed Tommy, "and it does look like Benjamin and Walter did it!"

"That's all very fine," commented Deborah, "but I doubt that an Enchanted Picture can be used as evidence in a court of law!"

"You are right," responded Glinda. "We must get evidence that would be legal in a court in the outside world! However, what we saw has proved to all of us that Joshua was murdered. This is the first step in getting his soul released to the afterlife."

"Unless I am mistaken," announced Deborah, "we have another ghost to contend with."

A surprised Tommy replied, "What?"

"Another ghost!" exclaimed Katie.

"Why yes!" continued Deborah. "Don't you remember the story I was telling you about the statue of Sarah? It told how on a night of a full-moon, her head would turn toward the lost mine!"

"Well, yes!" replied Katie and Tommy together.

"What do you think turned the head?" asked Deborah.

Tommy and Katie looked at each other. "We don't know!" they answered together.

"Would you believe Sarah's ghost turns the head?" suggested Deborah.

"Oh dear!" exclaimed Joshua, once more. "You mean my disappearance has made a ghost out of Sarah?"

"I am afraid that Deborah may be right!" declared Glinda. "Why don't we have the Enchanted Picture see what it can find out?"

With that, Glinda asked the Enchanted Picture to show the ghost of Sarah.

The normal peaceful picture disappeared once more. It was replaced by a picture of the lost graveyard on a full-moon light night. They could see George, the father of Katie and Tommy, sitting at the base of the statue in the lost graveyard, looking down toward the creek. The ghost of Sarah was visible and in the act of turning the statue head from pointing straight forward, to pointing in the direction of the lost mine.

"On my goodness!" cried Joshua. "You are right. Sarah is a ghost! Oh, what have I done?"

"Auntie!" shouted Katie. "Why is father sitting there by the statue?"

"He's probably out looking for us," replied Tommy.

"Well, at least he has made a good start!" answered Deborah. "He has found the lost graveyard. And Sarah is about to give him directions to the mine!"

"What's he holding in his hands?" asked Ozma.

"It looks like a Big Willies Peanut-butter and Jelly Bar wrapper," stated Katie. "You littered, brother!"

"And I suppose that isn't a box for Malt Flavored Chocolate Balls by his feet," added Tommy. "It looks like we both littered!"

"I think your father is glad that you did this one time," announced Glinda. "It does show him where you have been."

"Oh goodness!' explained Deborah. "I forget all about the flash flood we had. It would have washed away all our tracks."

"I am glad father was able to track us. I didn't think he could do that," remarked Tommy.

"Glinda!" requested Deborah. "Do you think we can help Sarah out as well as Joshua?"

"Don't worry about me!" pleaded Joshua. "Just help Sarah. She doesn't deserve to be a ghost. I drank too much and made bad business decisions. But she was good!"

"Deborah and Joshua," replied Glinda. "I am sure if we can solve Joshua's problem, then we will solve Sarah's problem as well!"

Chapter 16
A Visit to
Glinda's Castle

"I am sure that we can help Sarah by helping you, Joshua," continued Glinda. "So, the sooner we help you, the sooner we help Sarah. I think what we need is the advice of my Book of Records."

"Why don't we visit Glinda castle tomorrow?" suggested Dorothy. "That is, if you think Ozma wouldn't mind us going there."

"I am sure she would welcome anything we can do to help Joshua," replied Glinda. "However, Ozma is busy here in the Emerald City, so the rest of us will have to go without her!"

"Do you really think you can help Sarah and me?" inquired Joshua. "It has been so many years!"

"Well, you do have the loan of a body," stated Glinda.

"And you did get to eat food again!" remarked Deborah.

"The least that Glinda can do for Sarah is give her the loan of a body," suggested Katie.

"That way you and Sarah could be together again," added Tommy.

"That leaves one question," announced Katie. "Where do you live, Glinda?"

"Why I live at the southern edge of Oz," answered Glinda, "in Quadling Country. We can travel there tomorrow morning right after breakfast."

"That should give Joshua a chance to do something else he hasn't done for years," commented Deborah. "It is getting late and it is time for us humans to get some sleep."

"I don't know about that," remarked Joshua, "I don't think I can remember how to sleep."

"It's easy!" stated Tommy. "All you do is lay down on a comfortable bed, close your eyes, and rest."

"And before you know it," added Katie, "you will be dreaming about what you will do tomorrow."

"And what am I going to do tomorrow?" asked Joshua.

"Why, you are going to visit Glinda's castle and come up with a plan to get you justice!" responded Deborah.

So, everyone said good night to everyone else and went to their quarters to get some sleep.

Joshua tried hard to get some sleep, but he just couldn't seem to do it. Next, he started thinking about what he would like to do to his ex-partners. This kept his imagination busy for a while. Finally, he just thought about Sarah and all the problems he had caused her, and how he missed her. Before he knew it, a servant was waking him up for breakfast.

Everyone got up, got dressed, and had breakfast. After breakfast, they gathered in the courtyard. There was Glinda, the Wizard, Joshua, Deborah, Katie, Tommy, Joshua, Rocky, and Sigi.

Dorothy met them in the courtyard. Dorothy said, "I hope all of you had a good nights sleep. I think we will travel to Glinda's by carriage. With the Sawhorse pulling the carriage, it should be a fast trip."

So, everyone got into the carriage and headed for Quadling Country. With the Sawhorse given permission to travel at its best safe speed, it was a fast trip. Joshua watched the Emerald City, then fields of flowers fly by. He couldn't imagine such speed. This was followed by green fields.

Shortly, the scenery changed from the green color to a red tint. The grass and trees had a red tint. The houses were painted red. The carriage had crossed over into Quadling Country. Since they were traveling to the very edge of Oz, the trip took almost an hour. Finally the carriage came to a halt in the courtyard of Glinda's castle.

Glinda announced, "Welcome to my palace!"

Everyone got out of the carriage. The Wizard unhitched the Sawhorse.

Joshua requested, "Do you really think that you can help me find my eternal rest? How can we punish people who have already died?"

"Ah! Yes, your problem is most interesting," remarked Glinda. "I don't believe a two-hundred year-old murder has been solved before. But yes! I do believe we can help you, along with Sarah."

"Perhaps we could have a look in your magic book," suggested Dorothy. "It might give us some idea about the murder of Joshua and what happened around that time."

"Why not!" agreed Glinda. "I believe the magic book can fill us in on all that happened around Joshua's murder. Let us go to my private chamber and have a look at the book."

Everyone followed Glinda into her palace and then to her private chamber. In the middle of the chamber was an ebony stand. On it sat the magic book of Glinda's known as the Great Book of Records.

Glinda walked up to the book and opened it. She began to read aloud. "Early on the morning, in 1810 of the day of Joshua's death, Benjamin Black found a yellow streak in a coal vein at the end of a tunnel deep in the mine. He told Walter Flounder about it. The two of them were sure it was gold! Next, they talked about how it would be nicer to divide the wealth between the two of them rather than split it three ways. They decided to kill Joshua and bury him in the mine."

"Shortly thereafter, Benjamin and Walter took Joshua to the yellow streak in the coal vein." continued Glinda. "They told him that the three of them were rich, and that the yellow streak was gold! Joshua didn't believe them, but they all started to celebrate anyway. During the celebration, Joshua was killed by being stabbed in the back and hit in the head. He was buried at the cave-in down the first tunnel on the left. Later when Sarah went looking for Joshua, she was told that he had walked into the mine sometime ago and hadn't been seen since. The next day, Benjamin and Walter found out from some of their neighbors that the yellow streak was only sulfur, not gold. The murder had been pointless."

"Well, at least they didn't profit by my death!" remarked Joshua

"What can you do to prove that Joshua was murdered and to give him justice?" asked Tommy.

"I don't think our justice system can punish dead men!" exclaimed Katie.

"We would need to gather evidence that could be used in a court of law," stated Glinda. "Now my magic book and Ozma's Enchanted Picture cannot be used in a court of law. We used them to show you what happened so you would have an idea of where to get the evidence."

"Afterwards maybe we could have a trial here in the Land of Oz," suggested Dorothy, "that way we could clear Joshua's name."

"We could also find the guilty parties," injected Deborah. "While we cannot punish them, we can establish their guilt. Hopefully, that would be enough to get Joshua released to his eternal reward."

"And if Sarah can find out what actually happened," remarked Tommy.

"That would allow Sarah to go to her eternal reward too!" concluded Katie.

"To summarize, we need to gather evidence, have a trial, and find the guilty parties," stated Deborah, "and we will have to bring the evidence to Oz."

"We also need to bring the suspects to Oz," said Tommy.

"And don't forget to bring Sarah to Oz," added Katie. "She needs to see everything taking place!"

"Glinda! Can you bring Benjamin and Walter to Oz?" requested Dorothy. "I mean that they have been dead for two-hundred years. But I don't think that they are ghosts. I believe they went to their eternal reward!"

"That could be a problem," admitted Glinda. "We don't want to change history to any great extent, other then getting two ghosts released to their eternal reward, and we cannot interfere with the suspects' eternal reward."

"Perhaps we should see if we can find out what their eternal reward was?" suggested Dorothy.

"Maybe Glinda could look in her magic book and find out what happened to Benjamin and Walter?" requested Tommy.

"If Glinda can't do that, then I am sure Ozma's Enchanted Picture could show us the answers!" added Katie.

"Well, I think I should have another look in my magic book," agreed Glinda. She looked in the book and read the following information out loud. "Both Benjamin Black and Walter Flounder are having a very hot time in Hades. It seems that they are paying for their crimes for all eternity. So there is justice in the long term, but I do not have the power to bring them back from there to Oz for a trial."

"Oh, dear!" exclaimed Deborah. "How are we going to have a trial?"

"Can you bring them to Oz from the past?" suggested Tommy. "That is, can you bring them here while they were still alive?"

"If they are found guilty, maybe we could get them to make a deathbed confession of their crime?" added Katie.

"And that would give me justice and free my spirit to its eternal reward!" announced Joshua.

"Why, yes!" agreed Glinda. "I think that might be a workable plan. I can do most of the work with Ozma's magic belt. I will also arrange for Sarah's ghost to come to Oz and to get a temporary body."

Chapter 17
Making Plans
for the Trial

"I think the trial should be held at the palace in the Emerald City," suggested Dorothy. "However, the first thing we need to do is to decide on what we need for evidence?"

"As I recall," stated Deborah, "we need to prove the murderer had motive, method, and opportunity."

Tommy added, "True! But since this is a murder investigation, it would help if we have a corpse!"

Katie remarked, "A what?"

"A dead body," answered Deborah, "or if you prefer, a murder victim."

"The motive is easy to find," Joshua announced. "Benjamin Black and Walter Flounder didn't want to share the supposed gold in the coal seam!"

"The method of the murdered was to use a knife and a hatchet," commented Tommy.

"The opportunity occurred when the three of them were in the mine together at the end of the tunnel with the gold," remarked Katie.

"And the body or corpse can be found buried at the end of the first tunnel on the left!" stated Deborah.

"I can bring the body here, without any problems," assured Glinda. "It would be part of the evidence."

"Shouldn't we have some pictures taken at the coal mine, showing the discovery of the body?" suggested Tommy.

"I think that can be arranged," said the Wizard.

"And when you bring the body to Oz," continued Tommy, "the knife and hatchet would come with it. That would be the evidence showing the method used to kill Joshua."

"So, how do we prove motive and opportunity?" asked Katie.

"Well, we need to bring the gold in the coal seam to Oz," announced Deborah, "that is, if it still exists."

"That is something I can check on for you now," stated Glinda.

"And if it still exists, we need pictures of it showing it is still in the mine!" remarked Tommy. "Afterwards, we should bring some of it to Oz."

"I can take care of that as well if it still exists by using Ozma's Magic Belt," said Glinda. "But first, let me look in my book and find out about the gold."

So, Glinda looked in her book and read the following out loud. "Most of the gold in the coal seam at the end of one tunnel does still exist. Only a small part had been removed by Benjamin and Walker. They must have found out rather quickly that it was sulfur, not gold."

"Even if we bring the sulfur in the coal to Oz," commented Tommy, "it still doesn't prove the motive. What if they just say they knew it was sulfur?"

"But I was there and I heard them tell me it was gold!" cried Joshua. "I know they believed it!"

"However, you are the victim," insisted Katie. "You can't testify about your murder. You are dead and not a witness that can be used in court!"

"She has a good point!" announced Deborah. "How will we prove a motive?"

"It might help if we could get a confession out of Benjamin and Walter," suggested Katie.

"That's a very good suggestion," agreed Glinda.

"But how do we get the confession?" asked Tommy.

"Maybe I can haunt them a little," suggested Joshua. "You are going to bring them here while they were still alive, aren't you? Then I can haunt them as a ghost without violating the law."

"We can save that as a last resort," remarked Glinda. "Meanwhile, we must try to think of other ways to prove the motive."

"What about opportunity?" asked Deborah.

"If Joshua was killed in the mine," answered Glinda, "who had better opportunity then his fellow miners?"

"I just thought of another way to prove motive!" announced Tommy. "If we could get them to say that they ate lunch with Joshua, and then prove that Joshua didn't eat lunch, they would be caught lying! Why would they lie under oath unless they were covering up something?"

"Tommy!" exclaimed Katie. "That's a good idea! How do we prove Joshua didn't eat lunch?"

"Let me guess," suggested Deborah. "We need to do an autopsy on Joshua?"

"That just might be arranged," agreed Glinda.

"How about using the name of the mine as evidence?" inquired Katie. "The Black Hole Gold Mine does show that they didn't know much about mining. That would make it easier to believe that they might mistake sulfur for gold."

"That is very good, Katie," commented Tommy. "It is beginning to look like we do have a case against Benjamin and Walter."

"Who will be the judge for this case?" asked Joshua.

"Why Her Majesty, Ozma!" stated Dorothy. "It is part of her duties as the Ruler of the Land of Oz, to conduct all trials."

"And who will be the prosecutor?" asked Katie.

"Professor Woggle-Bug is the Public Accuser," announced Glinda. "He is so learned and no one can deceive him!"

"I think I want to help with the prosecution," requested Dorothy. "After all, I am a Princess of Oz."

"I think Ozma and Professor Woggle-Bug will agree to that," remarked Glinda. "I believe all of you can help with the prosecution."

"And who will be the defender?" asked Tommy.

"Now, that is a more difficult problem," remarked Dorothy. "We must provide Benjamin and Walter with the best defense possible. It will require someone with great intelligence to be the defender. That person should also have a kind heart!"

"How about the Scarecrow and the Tin Woodman?" recommended Glinda. "The Scarecrow has a magnificent brain and the Tin Woodman has a very kind heart."

"And they have had little to do with this case so far," stated Katie.

"That sounds fine," agreed Tommy. "Do we need a jury?"

"It is up to the defendants to decide if they want a jury or not," said Dorothy.

"That takes care of planning the trial," remarked Joshua. "Now, all we need to do is carry out our plans."

"Since most of the work will be done at Ozma's quarters in the Emerald City, I suggest we return there now," stated Dorothy, "that is, unless we have missed something."

"Perhaps you should stay for brunch," suggested Glinda.

"What's brunch?" asked Tommy.

"It's a meal halfway between breakfast and lunch," replied Katie. "Or, if you prefer, it is a meal combining breakfast and lunch."

"If you will follow me?" called Glinda. "I'll show you to my sitting room where brunch is being served."

Tommy was only too happy to follow Glinda. A meal by any other name was still a meal, and Tommy liked to eat. Everyone else also followed Glinda to her sitting room. There they found all sorts of cakes, pies, cookies, and other snack materials.

"Glinda!" remarked Joshua. "This is a real pleasure. I always had a sweet tooth."

"That's okay!" Glinda assured him. "You may also notice that the others are eating as well as you. Please enjoy yourself."

A few minutes later Glinda announced, "As soon as everyone has finished their brunch, you will be conducted to the courtyard."

"I don't know about the rest of you," stated Tommy, "but I am full."

"That'll be the day," teased Katie. "Tommy has never been full in his life!"

"I must say that the idea of eating brunch is new to me," said Joshua. "However, I think I could get used to it. Thank you, Glinda for inviting us to stay for brunch!"

"You're most welcome," replied Glinda. "I hope the rest of your stay in Oz is as much of a pleasure!"

"I am sure it will be, Your Majesty," answered Joshua.

"Well, now that the guest of honor is finished," suggested Deborah. "Why don't we all go out to the courtyard?"

After that remark, everyone went out to the courtyard. The Wizard hitched up the Sawhorse to the carriage. They thanked Glinda for her hospitality of her castle and then Glinda and the others got into the carriage. The Wizard acted as the driver and had the Sawhorse start out for the Emerald City.

Chapter 18
A Short Detour
on the Way

"Sawhorse!" requested the Wizard. "We want to go to the Emerald City. But . . ."

"I know, let me guess," interrupted the Sawhorse, "you want me to go slow enough so that you can watch the scenery!"

"Well, we do have guests with us," replied Glinda. "Deborah, Katie, Tommy, Joshua, and Rocky haven't seen much of Oz. So if it wouldn't inconvenience you too much, Sawhorse, would you go slowly?"

"For you, Glinda, I would do anything," replied the Sawhorse. The Sawhorse proceeded to pull the carriage slowly toward the Emerald City.

Since the carriage was passing through Quadling Country, the grass and trees had a red hue. All the houses that Dorothy and her friends passed were painted red. Most of the people wore red clothes.

"I must say that I have never seen so much red color before!" exclaimed Joshua. "Does everything in Quadling Country only come in the color red?"

"Why yes!" answered Dorothy. "It is one of the five major divisions of the Land of Oz. Each division has its own color. The Emerald City is green, Gillikin Country is purple, Munchkin Country is blue, Quadling Country is red, and Winkie Country is yellow. It makes it easier to tell where you are in the Land of Oz."

"It also helps you to tell where your food came from," added the Wizard. "You haven't tasted a good carrot until you try one of the purple carrots from Gillikin Country. They are very sweet!"

"And the blue potatoes from Munchkin Country are delicious!" stated Dorothy. "One could say that they are sweet potatoes."

The discussion of the various colors of fruits and vegetables of Oz, and how good they tasted, continued on for most of an hour.

"If we had Jim, the race horse, with us," commented Dorothy, "we could have him tell us which color grass tastes best. I do believe he preferred green grass."

"You had a race horse here in Oz with you, Dorothy?" asked Tommy.

"Oh, yes!" answered Dorothy. "Jim was a retired race horse that pulled the carriage for me and Cousin Zeb. Jim raced the Sawhorse, but it was no contest. The magical Sawhorse won the race easily."

"I believe I see a crossroads coming up," interrupted the Wizard. "Shall we stop and read the road signs?"

"Why, yes!" agreed Dorothy. "That sounds like a good idea."

"Sawhorse," called the Wizard. "If you wouldn't mind"

"I know, I know!" responded the Sawhorse. "Now you want me to stop! Well, why not!"

The Sawhorse stopped the carriage at the road sign.

"The sign says on our right, its one-half mile to China Country," read Dorothy out loud. "It's been a long time since I visited there. That was on my first trip to Oz."

"And what is China Country?" asked Joshua. "Do you have a Chinese settlement in Oz? No, let me guess. Chinese people would be too simple. I know! You have a country where the place settings of the table have come alive!"

"That is a good guess!" commented Dorothy. "However, I think I will just let you wait and see for yourself. Wizard, if you please."

"But, of course," replied the Wizard. "Sawhorse, we would like to visit China Country."

"What's a visit to China Country mean to me?" remarked the Sawhorse. "Nobody ever listens to me anyway."

With that, the Sawhorse turned to the right and headed for China Country. Within a couple of minutes, they were there.

There was a very high china wall surrounding China Country. At the end of the road, there was a door in the china wall. Next to the door was a door bell. A note had been attached to the door bell. The note said, "Please don't bother us. We are brittle and strangers tend to break us!"

"The first time I was here, I couldn't find the door," recalled Dorothy. "The Scarecrow, Cowardly Lion, Tin Woodman, and I climbed over the wall to get in and out of China Country."

"Perhaps this time we can use the door?" suggested the Wizard. "Tommy! Would you mind ringing the bell for us?"

"But the note says not to!" protested Tommy. "I don't want to make anyone mad at us, and I sure don't want to break someone!"

"I think if we are very careful, we can visit China Country without breaking anyone," Dorothy assured them. "Rocky, Sigi, and the Sawhorse will have to promise to stay with us at all times and to not bark or growl. And whatever else they do, they must not chase anyone! Is that understood?"

"Yes!" replied the Sawhorse, Sigi, and Rocky together.

"There will be no excuses!" said Dorothy. "Okay, Tommy! You can now ring the bell."

Tommy gave the bell a gentle push. Everyone waited for a moment or two. A strange man answered the door. He peered out carefully. He looked like a little figurine, made out of china and was only twelve inches tall.

"Can't you read?" called the china man. "We don't like visitors."

"Perhaps Her Highness, The Princess of China Country, could make an exception for us?" requested Dorothy. "Tell her Dorothy and her friends would like to see her."

"Dorothy and her friends?" questioned the china man. "I only know of one Dorothy. She is Princess Dorothy of Oz!"

"I am Princess Dorothy," proclaimed Dorothy.

"Your Highness!" replied the china man, as he gave a gentle bow. "I will inquire at once." The china man disappeared into China Country.

A minute or two went by, though it seemed much longer to those doing the waiting. Finally, the china man returned to the door.

"Her Highness says you and your friends are welcome, Your Highness!" announced the china man. "If you will follow me very carefully, Her Highness will see you. Please come this way, and do move slowly!"

"Please thank Her Highness for us," requested Dorothy. Dorothy, Glinda, the Wizard, Deborah, Katie, Tommy, and Joshua started moving very slowly behind the china man. Sigi, Rocky, and the Sawhorse were careful to stay in the middle of the group. The inhabitants of China Country backed away slowly from the strangers.

"Why is everyone afraid of us?" asked Tommy.

"The inhabitants of China Country are afraid of being broken or chipped," stated Dorothy. "If that happens, then they have to go to the mending shop. They never look quite as good after being mended as they did before the accident."

"That sounds like a very hard way to live!" remarked Katie. "They are always in fear. That's not good!"

"A little fear is healthy in that it makes them use caution," said Dorothy. "But yes, too much fear can make for a terrible life. However, too little fear is also bad!"

"I believe we can see how too little fear is a problem," continued Dorothy. "If we can find Mr. Joker, a clown, you will see what being broken in a hundred or more places can do to a china person."

During this talking, Dorothy and her group saw many of the inhabitants of China Country. They saw china milkmaids and cows. There were china shepherds and sheep. A china dog barked at them, but Sigi, Rocky, and the Sawhorse just ignored it. There were china buildings built on the same scale as the inhabitants. Everything was made out of china! Even the trees were china! The group was very careful to stay on the non-china walkway.

After a short walk, the group reached the palace of the China Princess. The palace was made out of china like everything else in China country. The China Princess and Her Court came out to meet Princess Dorothy and her party.

"Your Highness," greeted the Princess, "what a pleasure to see you and your friends. Is there something I can do for you?"

"Thank you, Your Highness," replied Dorothy. "Please, just call me Dorothy. May I introduce Deborah, her niece Katie, her nephew Tommy, her dog Sigi, Joshua, Rocky, the Sawhorse, and the Wizard?"

"It is a pleasure to meet all of you," responded Her Highness.

"Thank you, Your Highness!" answered everyone in the group.

"I wish to show my friends carefully around China Country," requested Dorothy. "Do you think it would be possible to see and talk with Mr. Joker, a clown?"

"We are honored to have you here as our guests," stated the China Princess. "Of course, you can have a slow and careful look around China Country, and I will send for Mr. Joker."

"Thank you, Your Highness," said everyone as the bowed to the Princess. The group was shown around China Country in a slow and careful manner. They saw the mending shop. They saw china Christmas trees and Christmas tree ornaments. There were china birds in the trees and china fish in the pond. Everywhere they looked were different kinds of china figurines. Most of the figurines were very beautiful, but some had been mended so often that they were no longer pretty. This was due to the many missing chips from the figurines. Some of the mended pieces took close inspection to see where they had been broken. All in all, the China Country was a very pretty place to visit.

As they were reaching the end of the tour, a messenger came carefully up to them.

"If you please, Dorothy," announced the china messenger. "We have located Mr. Joker. He has just been mended again! Oh, here he comes now!"

"Hello!" greeted Mr. Joker, as he tried to stand on his head. "Being mended many times had taken a toll on his balance. This time he was lucky and only fell over on his side, but nothing broke.

"Hello, Mr. Joker!" answered Dorothy. "It has been a long time since I last saw you. How are you doing?"

"My lady fair," began Mr. Joker in a rhythm.

"As you can see
I'm not afraid
to try anything.
And someday
as you will see
I'm going to succeed
at everything!" continued Mr. Joker.

"You can also see, I have been mended a number of times since we last met, but I am still trying to learn to stand on my head and maybe to turn cartwheels," stated Mr. Joker.

"You do show a great number of patches," agreed Tommy. "I would think you would learn to be more careful."

"I think the patches add character to my clown outfit," remarked Mr. Joker. "I am not afraid of anything. Well, it was nice seeing you. I've got to go practice standing on my head."

"Goodbye!" called Katie after Mr. Joker. "I've always liked clowns, and you are a very special clown. Good luck on your practicing!"

"I think we have seen enough of China Country," stated Dorothy. "Shall we return to the carriage?"

Everyone said goodbye to the inhabitants of China Country and they departed.

Chapter 19
Sarah Visits Oz

The Sawhorse continued traveling toward the Emerald City. Once he reached the Emerald City, he showed unusual care in moving through the streets on the way to the palace. Perhaps the trip to China Country had impressed him.

This time the crowds were smaller. It seems that Joshua as a man was not as interesting to look at as Joshua the ghost. Of course, the people did like to see Dorothy, the Wizard, and Glinda.

The group's progress got faster as the crowds thinned out. When the group arrived back at the palace, they gathered in Ozma's quarters. Ozma was not there because she was still busy with affairs of state for Oz. Everyone waited quietly for Glinda to activate Ozma's Enchanted Picture.

"Let us see Sarah's ghost," commanded Glinda, and the picture changed to show the lost graveyard once more. Sarah's ghost had just finished turning the head of the statue, making it point toward the lost mine. She was wondering why George was sitting at the base of the statue.

"So, the old stories are true," commented Tommy. "The ghost of Sarah does turn the statues head toward the lost mine on nights of a full-moon."

"Well, what did you expect, brother!" remarked Katie. "Most legends have some factual bases."

"Let me get Ozma's Magic Belt," announced Glinda, "then I will bring Sarah's ghost to Oz." With this, Glinda left the room for a moment. She came back in a minute and was wearing the Magic Belt. The Magic Belt was six inches wide and decorated with many large jewels.

"Magic Belt, let Sarah's ghost appear here before us!" commanded Glinda. The image of the ghost disappeared from the Enchanted Picture and suddenly Sarah's ghost was in their presence.

"Please don't be afraid," comforted Dorothy. "We are just trying to help you."

"I don't understand," replied the ghost of Sarah. "Where am I? What is happening? Who are you?"

"Iiiee, that is. I meeaaan!" stuttered Joshua. He was so happy to see and be with Sarah that he couldn't find words for the occasion.

Finally, Joshua managed to say, "You are in the Land of Oz, Sarah. We are here to solve my murder and to get you to your eternal reward."

"Oh, hello Joshua!" greeted Sarah. "I have almost forgotten what you looked like. Did you say you were murdered? If so, why aren't you a ghost? You sure don't look like a ghost! That is a mighty fine outfit that you are wearing. I don't think you have ever looked better."

"I have a temporary body, for use for finding my murderers," explained Joshua. "If you will go with these servants, you will be given a temporary body as well. That is, unless, of course, you don't want to find out what happened to me?"

"Joshua! You'll never learn," stated Sarah=s ghost. "I love you! Of course I want to know what happened to you." Sarah's ghost tried to give Joshua a hug, but her arms just went right through him.

"It is okay, Sarah!" Joshua assured her. "As a ghost, it is difficult to touch or move physical things, but I love you for just trying to hug me! Come along and we will see if we can't get you that body now! That will allow us to give each other a proper hug and kiss!"

So Sarah's ghost went with Joshua and the servants to Sarah's temporary quarters. There she was lent a body. Sarah and Joshua finally got to hug and kiss. Afterwards, Sarah and Joshua returned to the group in Ozma's quarters.

"Hello, everyone"" called a cheerful Sarah. "Do you like my new body? Oh Joshua! You are looking fine for being two-hundred years old!"

"Well, I know it's a long time," continued Sarah, who was enjoying having Joshua speechless. "Surely after two-hundred years, you should have thought of something to say to me! The least you can do hug me again."

Joshua gladly gave Sarah another hug. "It's been so long!" cried Joshua. "You can't imagine how I have missed you. Wow! That is a beautiful pink and white ball gown!"

"I have missed you for just as long as you missed me!" Sarah assured him. "Of course, I can imagine how you missed me. And your outfit looks good enough for church or a ball."

"At least you didn't go through the shock of being murdered!" stated Joshua.

"No, I didn't! However, I did go through the shock of not knowing what had happened to you!" responded Sarah. "All I knew was that you just walked into the mine and were never seen again!"

"Oh, my dear!" cried Joshua, "I know it was very bad for you. After all, you did die of a broken heart, two years later!"

"Perhaps Joshua and Sarah would like to spend some time alone to get to know each other all over again?" suggested Deborah.

"That's a good idea," agreed Glinda. "Joshua and Sarah, why don't you go to your quarters and get better acquainted?"

"Yes!" replied Sarah and Joshua together. So they went off to their quarters.

There in their quarters, Joshua played the host. He got the servants to bring in a light snack. Sarah got to eat her first food in two-hundred years.

"Wow!" remarked Sarah. "I never realized how much I enjoyed eating. This is really a treat! And I can enjoy smelling the food. I see flowers out in the courtyard. Can't we go smell them?"

"I don't see any reason why we shouldn't do that," answered Joshua. So, Joshua and Sarah went out to the courtyard and smelled and looked at the many different flowers.

"All this is great!" announced Sarah, after a few minutes. "And the air feels so good. I never thought I could experience these things again, but I am a ghost. Why am I getting to enjoy this? Why am I here?"

"You are here so that you can see me bring my murderers to justice," explained Joshua. "I helped Deborah and her friends when they were trapped in that old coal mine. So, now they are helping me to get justice. After that is accomplished, both you and I can stop being ghosts and go on to our eternal reward!"

"Who was that man sitting at the base of my statue, just before I came here?" asked Sarah.

"That was George Gilbert, the father of Katie and Tommy"" replied Joshua. "He is looking for Deborah, Katie, and Tommy. He doesn't know it yet, but you showed him how to find the lost mine. That is where Deborah, Katie, and Tommy got trapped by a cave-in."

"Oh dear!" remarked Sarah. "Poor George doesn't know that everyone is safe!"

"Don't worry too much about George!" stated Joshua. "I'm sure he will soon be successful at finding Deborah, Katie, Tommy, and Sigi. But you, Sarah, must have had a terrible time being a ghost and not knowing why you were a ghost."

"Well, I know it must have something to do with you, Joshua," explained Sarah. "And, of course, it had something to do with the mine. That's why my job was to rotate the statues head toward the lost mine on nights of a full-moon. However, you are right when you said I didn't know why I had to do this. When the mine entrance and graveyard got overgrown with weeds and brushes, I thought for sure that no one would ever discover them again!"

"Yes! That must have been a really scary thought," agreed Joshua, "waiting two-hundred years for someone to find the graveyard and lost gold mine. It was certainly a long wait, but it is finally about to end! And now that I've got to see you again, and I've got to talk to you, and even touch you, this is wonderful!"

Sarah and Joshua continued to talk with each other for over an hour. They were really enjoying each others company. About that time, Joshua had a thought.

"Perhaps it is time for us to rejoin the others?" suggested Joshua. "Then we can get on with solving my murder, so you and I can go to our eternal rest!"

"I guess that would be only fair of us," replied Sarah. "However, I am enjoying this so much that I am in no hurry to leave here! Besides, I don't want to take my hands off of you. You're so nice to have to hold."

"That's true," answered Joshua, "but we do have our duty to come to the end of our lives on earth. We are not to live forever. Our time has past. So, we must be willing to go on to our eternal reward."

"If you don't mind," requested Sarah, "how about one more kiss for the road?"

"Okay!" agreed Joshua. He kissed Sarah and then the two of them went back to Ozma's quarters. There they found the others discussing the plans for bringing Joshua's murderers to justice.

"Then it is agreed!" summarized Deborah. "First, we must gather all the physical evidence that we can. Then, we see if Her Majesty, Ozma, agrees we need a trial of Joshua's alleged murderers."

Chapter 20
Gathering the Evidence

"I think we should start by bringing Joshua's body to Oz," said Glinda. "It would be best if it was done within a few days of his murder; that way, the body will be in good enough condition for the Wizard to do an autopsy on it."

"Yes!" agreed Tommy. "The Wizard would need to see what was the last meal eaten by Joshua! If the defendants say they had lunch with him and the autopsy shows that his last meal was breakfast, then they must be lying!"

"We would also get the two murder weapons at the same time," added Katie.

"Unless I am mistaken," said Deborah, "Joshua will have to surrender his new body before we can bring his corpse here."

"But why?" asked Joshua.

"Because you can't be a dead person and also have a live body!" stated Sarah. "It just isn't done! That is why you will have to be a ghost again."

"Yes! That's right!" agreed Glinda. "Now, first we must send a photographer to the mine to photograph the evidence."

"Wizard!" continued Glinda. "How would you like to visit early Eastern Kentucky? While you are there, you can take the pictures we need for the evidence."

"I am sure that I would like that," responded the Wizard. "Let me see. I need to photograph the mines sign, the victim, and the sulfur in the coal seam."

"Would it help if I go along as a ghost?" asked Joshua. "I can help direct the Wizard as to where to find things."

"That sounds like a good idea," agreed Deborah.

"Perhaps a couple of nomes should be sent along to help with the digging?" added Dorothy.

"I will have Ozma send a request to the Nome King," stated Glinda.

"But won't all that take a lot of time!" objected Tommy.

"Not so long when you compare it to two-hundred years since the murder," remarked Katie.

"Even so," remarked the Wizard, "it will probably be tomorrow before we can get started on it."

"It just seems to take so long to get anything done!" exclaimed Tommy and Katie together.

"All that is true," agreed Deborah, "but we need to do everything correctly if we are to convict Joshua's murderers."

"I believe we also need to bring the Scarecrow, the Tin Woodman, and Professor Woggle-Bug to the Emerald City!" announced Glinda. "If they will be the defense and prosecution lawyers, then they should see our gathering of the evidence."

"But that would mean we can't surprise the defendants with the evidence!" complained Tommy.

"How are we going to shock the defendants into confessing if everyone knows what the evidence is before hand?" asked Katie.

"A court of law is a place to discover the truth!" stated Deborah. "The judge, the prosecutor, and the defender are all officers of the court. They are all trying to discover the truth!"

"So, why have defenders if all they are doing is trying to find out the true?" questioned Katie. "I thought he was there to find some improper methods used so the guilty person can go free!"

"The defenders are there to protect the rights of the defendants," acknowledged Deborah. "For this reason, the defenders may look harder for evidence that will clear the defendants. You really cannot expect the prosecutors to look for proof of innocence for the defendants."

"So the prosecutors tend to look for things that point to the defendants being guilty," suggested Tommy. "And the defender looks for things that would prove the defendants are innocent!"

"That's the idea," said Deborah. "That way, hopefully the whole true will be found!"

"Oh!" remarked Tommy and Katie together. "We didn't realize that both lawyers and the judge were all working toward the same goal."

"Since we are in agreement," said Glinda, "I will send a message to the Scarecrow, the Tin Woodman, and Professor Woggle-Bug. They should be here early tomorrow. Once they arrive, we will start gathering the evidence! Are there any questions?"

"No!" replied everyone.

"Sarah and Joshua!" said Deborah. "Since Joshua won't need to give up his body until tomorrow, why don't you two go off and have a quiet dinner together somewhere?"

"I like that idea," agreed Sarah. "Come along, Joshua. Let's see where we can find dinner."

"The idea is fine with me as well," added Joshua. "We'll see you folks later."

"That is about it!" stated Dorothy. "It seems we don't have anything to do until tomorrow. Why don't we go to my quarters and have a good dinner?"

"I don't know," remarked Tommy. "I'm not sure I can eat anything after all this excitement!"

"Don't worry, Dorothy!" Katie assured her. "I am sure Tommy will eat something. He has never turned down an offer of food in his entire life."

"Wizard and Glinda!" requested Dorothy. "Would you like to join us for dinner?"

"Well I guess I can spare a little time for dinner," replied the Wizard, "however, after dinner I should see about getting my cameras ready for tomorrow."

"I think I need to talk with Ozma," responded Glinda. "I will see you later."

So Dorothy, the Wizard, Deborah, Katie, Tommy, Rocky, and Sigi headed for Dorothy's quarters. Here the servants had prepared a fancy meal. Everyone ate all that they wanted. Afterwards, they all managed to have a little dessert.

As the group was finishing dessert, Glinda came by. Everyone looked at her, trying to tell what she had found out.

"Oh good!" said Glinda. "I always like having a little dessert. Do you mind if I join you?"

"Of course, we want you to join us," replied Dorothy. "Please come in and have a seat. Help yourself to some dessert." So Glinda helped herself to a slice of Oz pie.

"The Scarecrow, Tin Woodman, Professor Woggle-Bug will be here in the morning," said Glinda between bites of the pie. "The Scarecrow and Tin Woodman have agreed to represent Benjamin and Walter in this case. They will be going with the Wizard and Joshua."

"Great!" replied the Wizard. "Now if you will excuse me, I have some cameras I need to prepare for tomorrow."

"Perhaps it is time we all think about going to bed," suggested Deborah. "I don't know about the rest of you, but I have had several busy days. I can use some sleep."

"We agree, Auntie!" replied Katie and Tommy together. So, everyone said good night to everyone else and went to their own quarters. Soon, everyone was fast asleep, but the Wizard. He was busy checking on the technical details for tomorrows activities.

The next morning, everyone hurried through getting dressed and having breakfast. Afterwards, they all met at Ozma's quarters. Glinda joined them. Ozma had to leave and work on affairs of state.

The Scarecrow, Tin Woodman, the Wizard, and Professor Woggle-Bug joined the group in Ozma's quarters. The Gilberts got their first good look at the Woggle-Bug when he was introduced to them.

Deborah just stared at the Woggle-Bug with her mouth open.

"Oh my!" exclaimed Katie. "You are a BIG bug!"

"He is the biggest bug I have ever see!" agreed a curious Tommy. "Are there others like you?"

"I am Professor H. M. Woggle-Bug, T. E.," stated the Professor. "The H. M. stands for Highly Magnified and the T. E. for Thoroughly Educated. As far as I know, I am the only woggle-bug with H. M. and T. E. Most woggle-bugs are tiny little bugs."

"We are happy to meet you, Professor," announced Deborah after she recovered from her shock of first seeing the large bug.

"I have never seen such a large bug, who wears clothes, and talks," remarked Tommy. "I am Glad to meet you."

"That goes for me too," added Katie.

The first thing Glinda needed to do was to change Joshua back to a ghost. So, after Joshua kissed Sarah goodbye, he and Glinda went into another room. When they returned, Joshua was a ghost once more.

"Oh dear!" exclaimed Sarah, just a little shocked. "I didn't know you were such a scary ghost. That knife and hatchet are awful!"

"I am sorry you have to see me this way," apologized Joshua, "but you know this is necessary."

"I know!" agreed Sarah. "Goodbye for now, and good luck."

Next, Glinda sent the Wizard, the Scarecrow, the Tin Woodman, and Joshua back to two days after his murder by using Ozma's Magic Belt. She also sent several nomes to the mine as well. There the nomes carefully uncovered the body of Joshua. The Wizard took pictures and the Scarecrow witnessed everything. Next, the Wizard took pictures of the mines sign. Finally, he had the nomes show him the coal seam with the sulfur deposits in it and took pictures of it.

"That should do it!" announced the Wizard into seemingly empty air. "We are ready to transfer the evidence to my lab in Oz."

This Glinda did by using Ozma's Magic Belt. She brought the Wizard, Joshua, the Tin Woodman, and the Scarecrow back to Oz.

After the nomes had carefully removed all traces of anyone being in the mine, Glinda sent them back to their home.

"Well, we now have the evidence," stated the Wizard. "If the Scarecrow and Tin Woodman will accompany me, I will go do the autopsy."

"Let's get it over with!" remarked the Scarecrow. He wasn't sure that he would enjoy that part.

The rest of them waited not so patiently in Ozma's quarters. Everyone wanted to know what the Wizard would find. The waiting went on for two hours. Everyone was very nervous by then. Finally, the Wizard, Tin Woodman, and the Scarecrow returned to Ozma's quarters.

"Well, what did you find out?" asked Deborah, impatiently.

"I will tell you in a moment," responded the Wizard. "However, first we need to ask Sarah something!"

"What do you want to know?" replied Sarah.

"Do you know what you fixed for Benjamin, Walter, and Joshua's lunch on the day of Joshua's disappearance?" requested the Wizard.

"There were some bread, sausage, and some carrots," recalled Sarah. "We didn't have much money, so we didn't eat very fancy."

"And one final question," added the Wizard. "What did Joshua have for breakfast?"

"That's easy," answered Sarah. "We always had porridge with fruit on the side, and I think we also had eggs that morning."

"Excellent! That's all I needed to know! Joshua was murdered. And he didn't eat lunch!" summarized the Wizard.

"Well, that takes care of all our evidence," commented Deborah.

Chapter 21
Benjamin and
Walter Brought to Oz

"Now the Scarecrow and I must take all the evidence to Her Majesty, Ozma, at her throne room," stated the Woggle-Bug. "Then, if Her Majesty, that is Ozma, thinks the evidence warrants it, she can issue warrants for the arrest of Benjamin Black and Walter Flounder. Meanwhile, why don't the rest of you wait in Dorothy's quarters?"

"Yes, we must have warrants before we arrest Benjamin and Walter," agreed the Scarecrow. "Otherwise, we would be breaking the law ourselves. That won't be good."

So the Scarecrow and the Woggle-Bug went to the throne room. Here Ozma acted as the judge and the Scarecrow and the Woggle-Bug presented all their evidence of the crime. Ozma listened to their presentations and finally asked the Scarecrow and Woggle-Bug to come back in an hour. During that time, she would consider the evidence and then give her decision.

The Woggle-Bug and the Scarecrow went back to Dorothy's quarter to wait out the hour. There they explained to everyone what was happening. Everyone just paced up and down the room for the rest of the hour.

When the time was up, the Woggle-Bug and the Scarecrow went back to the throne room to see Ozma. Ozma was waiting for them.

"I have considered all the evidence," stated Ozma. "It does look like a crime may have been committed. And the evidence does suggest that Benjamin Black and Walter Flounder may have committed the crime."

"Therefore," continued Ozma, "it is my duty to issue arrest warrants for Benjamin Black and Walter Flounder. You may have the Oz army help you with the arrest. I will recall a couple of the officers to active duty. An army officer will bring you the warrants as soon as they are issued!"

"Thank you, Your Majesty!" said the Woggle-Bug. The Scarecrow and Woggle-Bug bowed and left Her Majesty's presence. They hurried back to Dorothy's quarters.

"Well? What happened?" asked Deborah for everyone present.

"Her Majesty is issuing arrest warrants for Benjamin and Walter," answered the Woggle-Bug. "When they arrive, we can bring Benjamin and Walter to Oz and have them arrested."

"Of course, from this point on," added the Scarecrow, "Benjamin and Walter will be mine and Nick's clients. We will therefore be doing everything in our power to clear them of this ridiculous charge!"

Tommy exclaimed, "What?"

"It is okay brother! It is now the Scarecrow's duty to protect the rights of Benjamin and Walter. Remember that we all want to find out the truth!" Katie reminded Tommy.

"I guess so," admitted Tommy. "I just don't know if I trust lawyers."

"Please understand, for it to be a fair trial, the accused must have the best defense possible!" explained Deborah.

The group waited around for the warrants to arrive. It took about one-half hour. Finally, two Oz army officers knocked on Dorothy's door.

"Who is it?" asked Deborah, as she opened the door.

"It is a Major and a Captain of the Oz army," answered the Major. "I have the warrants you requested from Her Majesty. We have also been instructed to assist you in any way we can."

"Well, come on in," replied Deborah.

The officers came into Dorothy's quarters. They handed Dorothy the warrants. Dorothy read the warrants and handed it to the Scarecrow. The Scarecrow then read the warrants.

"Do the warrants look in order, Scarecrow?" asked Dorothy.

"They look fine to me!" replied the Scarecrow.

"Now we can get on with the arrest of Benjamin and Walter" replied Deborah. "Let's go to Ozma's quarters and get things started."

So, everyone went to Ozma's quarters. They gathered around the Enchanted Picture in Ozma's sitting room.

"We don't want to interfere with history," said Glinda. "That is, we don't want to make any major changes to it. Both Benjamin and Walter have long since been dead, and we cannot do anything that will greatly alter their lives."

"So, that is why we need to bring them to Oz during a time when they were still alive!" remarked Deborah. "It should also be a time while Sarah was still alive. That way she could be a witness at the trial."

"It should be a time when they are alone!" suggested Tommy. "That would limit the possibility of changing their lives."

"But I am sure they will be surprised!" added Katie.

"Okay, then!" began Glinda. "Let us first locate Benjamin within two years of Joshua's death. Enchanted Picture would you please show me Benjamin Black."

The Enchanted Picture then changed to show Benjamin Black asleep in bed, by himself.

"This should do very nicely," said Glinda. "Just let me get Ozma's Magic Belt!" So Glinda left the room for a moment. When she returned, she was wearing the Magic Belt.

"Let Benjamin Black be brought here to Oz from his own time," commanded Glinda. Within a few seconds, Benjamin Black landed in the middle of Ozma's sitting room.

The Enchanted Picture now showed the sitting room of Ozma's quarters.

"What the.... Where am I?" asked Benjamin Black, as he stared at the strangers around him. "Why am I here?"

"Are you Benjamin Black?" asked the Army Major. "That is the Benjamin Black who was once a partner in a mine with Walter Flounder and Joshua Smith?"

"Well yes I am, but whaaa..." Benjamin tried to say.

"Then, in the name of Ozma, the Ruler of the Land of Oz," continued the Major, "I arrest you for the murder of Joshua Smith!"

"But I never heard of a Land of Oz!" exclaimed Benjamin. "What right do you have to arrest me?"

"All of that will be explained to you!" assured the Major. "For now I must ask you to come along with us." So, the officers took hold of Benjamin and took him out of Ozma's quarters. They took him to a holding cell.

"You will wait here!" commanded the Major. "Servants will bring you some clothes. If you need anything else, ask the servants."

"I think I need a lawyer!" stated Benjamin.

"Your lawyers will be along in a few minutes!" responded the Major. "Please just be patient. I am sure they can explain things to you."

"Now that I would like to see!" shouted an angry Benjamin. "What are your name, rank, and serial number? I think I will sue you for false arrest!"

"Your lawyers will have all that information for you," replied the Major. "For now, all you can do is just sit and wait here."

Finally, the Major and Captain returned to Ozma's quarters. "That is one of the defendants in custody," announced the Major. "Now what do you want us to do?"

"You just need to do is wait patiently," replied Glinda. "Now we will try to get Walter for you."

"Enchanted Picture," requested Glinda, "Please shows us Walter Flounder, when he is alone, sometime in the two years following Joshua's death!"

The Enchanted Picture changed from showing Benjamin in his cell to showing Walter in bed by himself.

"This seems to be working out very well!" remarked Glinda. "Let Walter Flounder be brought from his own time to Oz."

Within a few seconds, Walter Flounder landed in the middle of Ozma's sitting room.

The Enchanted Picture once again showed Ozma's sitting room.

"That will be all," commanded Glinda to the Enchanted Picture. The Enchanted Picture then switched to showing an ordinary picture.

"What's going on here?" demanded Walter. "Who are you? Where am I?"

"You will know in a minute," replied the Major, "but first I need to know if you are the Walter Flounder that once was a partner in a mine with Joshua Smith and Benjamin Black?"

"I don't know what you are talking about," stated Walter. "There must be some kind of mistake!"

"Oh, it is Walter Flounder, all right," announced Sarah. "I would remember him forever!"

"In that case," said the Major, "I hereby arrest you, Walter Flounder, for the murder of Joshua Smith!"

"Don't be ridiculous!" screamed Walter. "I tell you. You have the wrong man!"

"Officers, if you please!' commanded Glinda.

"By your command," responded the Major. They took Walter to the holding cell next to Benjamin.

"Okay, now, that's done!" announced Glinda. She left the room and removed her magic belt. Then she returned to the sitting room.

"Scarecrow and Tin Woodman!" said Deborah. "I believe you have two clients to see."

"Oh yes! Most assuredly," replied the Scarecrow. "I must go to them at once. I don't want any of their rights violated!"

The Scarecrow left immediately for the cells of Benjamin and Walter.

"Wait for me!" called the Tin Woodman after the Scarecrow.

"I think that takes care of the business for this morning," remarked Dorothy. "I think we should give Joshua's ghost, Sarah, and the others a chance to look around the Emerald City. When you are finished, we can have lunch."

"That's fine," agreed Glinda. "Please don't forget that everyone is to be at the throne room at two o'clock this afternoon."

"Why?" asked Tommy.

"So that we can watch the hearing for Benjamin and Walter," replied Deborah.

"You mean the trial, don't you, Auntie?" asked Katie.

"No!" answered Deborah. "After Benjamin and Walter have a talk with their lawyers, and see the evidence against them, we have to have a hearing. It will determine if there is enough evidence to rate a trial."

"And if there isn't enough evidence. What happens then?" questioned Tommy.

"Then the case will be dismissed against them!' responded Glinda.

"Would that mean we lose?" asked Katie.

"That's about the size of it!" answered the Wizard. "Therefore, I think the Woggle-Bug, Dorothy, and I should go review all the evidence and prepare our case against Benjamin and Walter!"

So everyone said goodbye. Each went off on their own.

Chapter 22
The Hearing

Glinda, Deborah, Tommy, and Katie were sitting in the throne room, with Sarah awaiting the arrival of Her Majesty, Ozma. At the Defenders' table sat Benjamin and Walter, along with their lawyers, the Scarecrow and the Tin Woodman. At the Prosecutors' table sat the Woggle-Bug, Dorothy, and the Wizard. The Bailiff was one of the Oz army officers.

"All rise," called the Bailiff. "This court of Oz is now called to order. Her Majesty, Ozma, is presiding."

Ozma entered the room from behind the throne. She then sat herself on the throne. "You may all be seated!" announced Ozma. "Bailiff, what case do we have before us?"

"Your Majesty," replied the Bailiff, we have the state versus Benjamin Black and Walter Flounder."

"And what does the state accuse them of?" requested Ozma.

"Your, Majesty, the state accesses Benjamin Black and Walter Flounder of killing Joshua Smith!" stated the Woggle-Bug.

"Are the defendants represented by council?" asked Ozma.

"Yes they are, Your Majesty," answered the Scarecrow. "I and the Tin Woodman are representing them. We are ready to hear the evidence against them."

"And is the state ready to present the evidence?" inquired Ozma.

"Yes, we are, Your Majesty," replied the Woggle-Bug. "We believe that there is sufficient evidence to justify bringing Benjamin Black and Walter Flounder to trial for the murder of Joshua Smith!"

"If all parties are ready then let the state present its evidence!" commanded Ozma.

"The defendants are accused of murdering Joshua Smith in 1810, in Eastern Kentucky," began the Woggle-Bug. "As evidence of the crime, we have Joshua Smiths body with a knife stuck in his back and a hatchet buried in his head. The body was found at the end of the first tunnel on the left of a coal mine owned and operated by Joshua, Benjamin, and Walter."

"Benjamin and Walter had the opportunity to kill Joshua," continued the Woggle-Bug. "Their motive was to keep his share of the mine profits. The method was using a knife and hatchet! We have photographs of all the evidence."

Dorothy took the photographs up to Her Majesty, Ozma. Ozma looked very carefully at the photographs.

"And what do the defendants have to say about this?" asked Ozma.

The Scarecrow got up. "Your Majesty," began the Scarecrow. "The defendants say that this is all a great misunderstanding. Benjamin, Walter, and Joshua were not only business partners in the mine but also were the best of friends. While it is clear that Joshua was killed, my clients did not do it. In fact, there was no murder!"

"No murder!" exclaimed Ozma. "Then what does this picture of a body show?"

"That picture shows that Joshua was killed and how he died," stated the Scarecrow. "However, Joshua died of an accident of his own making. It was just a terrible accident. If my clients are guilty of anything, it is trying to keep Sarah from finding out that Joshua accidentally killed himself!"

From among the spectators, Sarah shouted, "What? How in the world did Joshua stab himself in the back and bury a hatchet in his head?" At this point there was much talking by the others present in the room.

"Order please! We will have order in this court!" demanded Ozma. "Young lady, you can't just shout out things like that. Do you understand? Don't do it again!"

"Yes Your Majesty!" replied Sarah. "I am sorry, but I don't believe their story."

"That is why we are here today," explained Ozma. "We wish to determine if there is sufficient evidence to justify trying these persons for the murder of Joshua Smith. However, I must admit that I am wondering what their whole story will be like."

"Now, Scarecrow," continued Ozma. "Are your clients saying that they knew about the death of Joshua?"

"Yes Your Majesty!' responded the Scarecrow.

"And that they covered up his death to protect Sarah?" added Ozma.

"Yes Your Majesty!" answered the Scarecrow. "However, they now see that the cover up was not a good idea!"

"I should say not!" remarked Ozma.

"There is one more thing, Your Majesty," stated the Scarecrow. "Not only are my clients innocent, but they were kidnapped and brought to Oz illegally. Therefore, Your Majesty, I move that my clients be set free and returned to their own world. In addition, I think the agents of the state should be charged with kidnapping!"

"I object!' exclaimed the Woggle-Bug. "The defendants were brought here legally at Her Majesty's request."

Once again the spectators were in an uproar. No one could quite believe their ears.

"Order please! Order! We will have order in this court or the room will be cleared of all spectators!" announced Ozma.

"The prosecutions objection is noted!" continued Ozma. "I issued the warrant for the arrest of the defendants. It was perfectly legal."

"As for this case," explained Ozma, "we believe that there is sufficient evidence to justify holding the defendants for a trial. When can the state and defender be ready for the trial?"

"I think that a speedy trial is in order," replied the Tin Woodman. "If it is all right with the Woggle-Bug, my clients can be ready for trial tomorrow!"

"Does the state object?" asked Ozma.

"No Your Majesty!" replied Woggle-Bug. "We can be ready for trial by tomorrow. We think that a speedy trial will benefit all the parties in this case."

"Very well," ruled Ozma. "I hereby command that the defendants be held over for trial on the murder of Joshua Smith. The trial will begin at ten o'clock tomorrow morning. Court adjourned."

"All rise!" cried the Bailiff. Everyone rose. Her Majesty then left the room by way of a passage behind the throne.

'What do we do now?" asked Tommy.

"We go to Dorothy's quarters and see if we can help her and the Woggle-Bug prepare their case against Benjamin and Walter," replied Deborah.

"So, this wasn't a trial?" questioned Katie.

"Why, no!" answered Deborah. "It was just a hearing to determine if the evidence warrants a trial. Her Majesty, Ozma, thinks that it does. So tomorrow, Benjamin and Walter will stand trial for the murder of Joshua."

"Then what happens?" inquired Tommy.

"If they are found guilty, they will be punished!" stated Deborah.

"But how can we punish them?" asked Katie.

"That will be up to Her Majesty to decide," responded Dorothy. Dorothy really didn't know how one could punish people who were already dead, but she kept her thoughts to herself.

Dorothy and the others got together for dinner in her quarters. She had also invited the Scarecrow, the Tin Woodman, the Woggle-Bug, the Wizard, and Jack Pumpkinhead to dinner. Poor Joshua was still a ghost so he couldn't eat food. No one else seemed to be interested in dinner either. It wasn't that the food was bad; it was just that everyone was concerned about how the trial would go. If things didn't go well, then Joshua would remain a ghost forever.

"Well, we are grateful that Joshua has shown us what he looked like as a ghost," remarked the Tin Woodman. "He is quite different!"

"Yes!" agreed Jack. "We missed his ghost act earlier. Thank you, Joshua, for showing us your ghostly image. However, we do not want Joshua to be a ghost forever!"

"I am against Joshua being a ghost forever too!" stated the Scarecrow. "But if that is caused by my clients being innocent, then that is just the way it will be. I will do my best to defend them."

"We expect you and the Tin Woodman to do nothing less, Scarecrow!' Dorothy assured him. "That is why you were chosen for their lawyers. You two do have the best brain and heart in Oz."

"So, if you can't prove that your clients are innocent, they must be guilty," commented Tommy.

"No! Tommy!" corrected Deborah. "We must prove them guilty. Even if the Scarecrow can't prove them innocent, it doesn't mean that we can prove them guilty beyond a reasonable doubt. We must prove them guilty, or they go free!"

"All of us expect you to do your best to defend them, Scarecrow and Tin Woodman!" explained Katie. "We think that you are their best hope!"

"Well, since no one seems to be interested in dinner," announced Deborah, "why don't we all go to our own quarters and think about what, if anything, we need to do before the trial tomorrow!"

Everyone thought this was a good idea. So they said good night and returned to their own quarters.

There was much thinking going on that night. Dorothy and all her friends were trying to review the evidence in their heads. They were trying to remember if they had missed anything.

No one slept well that night. Each person was seeing in his or her mind the events of the murder over and over. Had any details missed their attention?

Joshua was a ghost again. He didn't need any sleep. So he wandered around the palace all night. He visited the Wizard who was busy looking over his autopsy report. The Scarecrow was with him and reviewed all the evidence.

At Sarah's quarters, Joshua made his presence know. Sarah was pleased to see him, but she was worried that he might have to remain a ghost forever. She wasn't sure whether she would once more become a ghost or not. After all, she now knew what happened to Joshua. At least that much good had come out of all this.

Next, Joshua visited Dorothy. She was busy double checking all the facts.

Last of all, Joshua visited Benjamin and Walter in their cells. "Remember me!" called Joshua to each of them. "I am the ghost of Joshua Smith. You killed me!" Both Benjamin and Walter seemed to be asleep. Joshua didn't know if they heard him.

Chapter 23
The Trial

The next morning, everyone got up, got dressed, and had breakfast alone. Once again, no one seemed that interested in eating, but they manage to eat a little something just to keep up their strength.

After breakfast, Katie, Tommy, Sarah, and Joshua gathered in Deborah's quarters. Shortly thereafter, the Woggle-Bug, Dorothy, and the Wizard joined them.

"Sarah!" said the Wizard. "Would you be willing to testify at the trial? I could use you to tell them what you prepared for Joshua's breakfast and lunch on the day of his disappearance."

"Of course, I will," replied Sarah. "I'll do anything to help Joshua."

"I think it might be necessary if Benjamin and Walter don't stick to the truth!" continued the Wizard. "We will just have to wait and see. I think I have everything ready for the trial. So I think the best thing we can do is just relax until ten o'clock."

"That is good advice," stated Dorothy. "We will all meet at ten o'clock at the throne room." Everyone agreed to the suggestion, so everyone was on their own until ten o'clock.

At ten minutes before ten o'clock, everyone met at the throne room. Tommy was carrying a book and a bag with an ore sample in it. These he gave to Dorothy with a short explanation. Dorothy then went off to discuss the items with the Scarecrow and the Woggle-Bug. When Dorothy returned, they all went inside and took their places. Shortly thereafter, the Bailiff called the court to order.

"The next case is the Land of Oz verses Benjamin Black and Walter Flounder," announced the Bailiff. "They are accused of killing Joshua Smith."

"Is the defense ready?" asked Her Majesty, Ozma.

"We are, Your Majesty!" replied the Scarecrow.

"Is the State ready?" requested Ozma.

"We are, Your Majesty!" replied the Woggle-Bug.

"Will the defendants please rise?" asked Ozma.

The Scarecrow and the Tin Woodman stood up with his clients, Benjamin and Walter.

"How do the defendants plea? Guilty or not guilty?" asked Ozma.

"They plead not guilty, Your Majesty!' responded the Scarecrow.

"Do the defendants wish to have a jury?" inquired Ozma.

"No Your Majesty," announced the Tin Woodman. "Our clients wish for you to decide the case. They know you will give them justice!"

"In that case," continued Ozma, "will the Prosecution give its opening statement."

The Woggle-Bug stood and said, "We, the State of Oz, will show that Benjamin Black and Walter Flounder did willfully kill Joshua Smith. This premeditated act took place in 1810, in a mine they owned in Eastern Kentucky! We will show that they had means, motive, and opportunity. We will prove that Benjamin and Walter are guilty of first degree murder!" Then the Woggle-Bug sat down.

"Can we now have the opening statement for the defense?" requested Ozma.

The Scarecrow stood. "Your Majesty," began the Scarecrow. "We will prove that it was all a terrible accident! Joshua was a drunkard! He caused his own death. My clients were upstanding citizens of their community. They were Joshua's best friends. When they found Joshua's body, after his accident, they hid the body to protect Sarah Smith from learning about the terrible death. If the truth were known, Sarah would have become an outcast of the community!" At this point, the Scarecrow sat down. "The only thing they are guilty of was trying to protect a friend's reputation."

"Is the prosecution ready to present its case?" inquired Ozma.

"We are, Your Majesty," replied the Woggle-Bug. "I wish to have the following photographs placed in evidence and tagged exhibit A, Your Majesty. They show the name of the mine, at its entrance, as being THE BLACK HOLE GOLD MINE, and some ore at the end of one of the shafts."

"We have no objections, Your Majesty!' responded the Scarecrow.

"In addition, we also have the mine sign here," continued the Woggle-Bug. "Please label it exhibit B."

"No objection, Your Majesty!" responded the Scarecrow.

"And we would like to have this ore sample tagged as exhibit C!" finished the Woggle-Bug.

"No objections, Your Majesty," said the Scarecrow once again.

"What do you mean by no objections?" asked Benjamin and Walter together. "What are they up to?"

"They are trying to prove a motive for the alleged murder," replied the Scarecrow.

"So, what do we do now?" asked Walter.

"We wait until they try to explain the meaning of the evidence," stated the Scarecrow. "We cannot dispute the existence of the physical evidence, but we can dispute their explanation of its meaning."

"Your Majesty," continued the Woggle-Bug. "I will be calling witnesses separately for each part of the prosecution. That is, to show motive, opportunity, and method. I would like to have the Wizard called as a witness to explain the meaning of this evidence. It will show that Benjamin and Walter had a motive for killing Joshua."

"The court calls the Wizard," announced Ozma.

The Wizard moved to the witness chair.

"Do you promise to tell the truth, the whole truth, and nothing but the truth?" asked the Bailiff.

"I do!" answered the Wizard.

"Wizard, did you gather the evidence and take these pictures?" requested the Woggle-Bug.

"Yes, I did," replied Wizard. "The Scarecrow, Tin Woodman, and I together visited the BLACK HOLE GOLD MINE and gathered the evidence!"

"What kind of mine does the sign say that it is?" asked the Woggle-Bug.

"Why, it is a gold mine," responded the Wizard.

"And what would people digging in a gold mine be looking for?" inquired the Woggle-Bug.

"Objection!" called the Scarecrow. "It calls for a conclusion from the witness."

"Overruled!" stated Ozma. "The mines name doesn't require an expert to guess what the people were digging for. You may answer the question, Wizard."

"Yes Your Majesty!" replied the Wizard. "They were looking for gold!"

"I see you brought an ore sample with you, Wizard!" continued Dorothy. "What is so special about it?"

"Objection!" cried the Scarecrow. "The Wizard has not been qualified as a mining expert!"

"Your Majesty," stated the Woggle-Bug. "We don't want an expert opinion. We want to know what a non-expert sees in the ore. If we need an expert witness, we will call a nome."

"Objection overruled," announced Ozma. "Please answer the question."

"Well, as you can see, there is a yellow streak in this ore sample," continued the Wizard. "To an inexperienced miner, this could be taken for gold! It has happened before."

"Objection!" shouted the Scarecrow. "Where is the relevance? My clients were experienced miners."

"I doubt that, Your Majesty!" exclaimed the Woggle-Bug. "If they were experienced miners, they wouldn't be looking for gold in a coal mine."

"Your objection is noted, Scarecrow!" acknowledged Ozma. "You may build on it during your cross examination of this witness. Does the prosecution have any other references to back up this idea of no gold in a coal mine?"

"If it pleases Your Majesty," said the Woggle-Bug, "may I refer the court to the section on fool's gold in the Oz Encyclopedia. We can call it exhibit D, and this ore sample as exhibit E."

"No objections, Your Majesty!" replied the Scarecrow.

"So, what does all this suggest in the way of a motive?" asked the Woggle-Bug of the Wizard.

"That Benjamin, Walter, and Joshua found this yellow streak in the coal seam and thought it was gold. Finally, Benjamin and Walter killed Joshua so they wouldn't have to split the profits three ways!"

"Your witness!" called the Woggle-Bug to the Scarecrow.

"Let us assume that Benjamin, Walter, and possibly Joshua thought this yellow streak was really gold. When did they find it? What is the yellow stuff?" asked the Scarecrow.

"The yellow streak is sulfur," replied the Wizard. "I tested some of it in my laboratory. However, I don't know when it was discovered."

"I am through with this witness!" announced the Scarecrow. "However, I do reserve the right to recall him later!"

"Very well!" agreed Ozma. "The witness may step down for now, but stay available to the court."

The Wizard stepped down.

"I wish to call Sarah Smith," stated the Woggle-Bug.

"The court calls Sarah Smith!" said Ozma.

Sarah came forward and got into the witness chair.

"Do you promise to tell the truth, the whole truth, and nothing but the truth?" asked the Bailiff.

"I do!" replied Sarah.

"Sarah!" said the Woggle-Bug. "Did your husband ever tell you about what they found in the mine?"

"Yes!" answered Sarah. "He told me at the end of every day about what they had done and found in the mine that day."

"And did he ever tell you about finding a yellow streak in the coal?" continued the Woggle-Bug.

"Why no!" answered Sarah.

"And how do you account for that?" requested the Woggle-Bug.

"Objection!" called the Scarecrow. "It asks the witness to make a conclusion!"

"Overruled!" stated Ozma. "Please answer the question."

"Why, I guess he didn't tell me about the yellow streak in the coal, because they hadn't found it yet!" answered Sarah.

"So, before the day of Joshua's death," summarized the Woggle-Bug, "they hadn't found the yellow streak, or Joshua would have told you."

"That's right," agreed Sarah. "Joshua always told me everything about what he did that day. He even told me about his work on his still!"

"Your witness!" said the Woggle-Bug to the Scarecrow.

"Joshua always told you about his work!" repeated the Scarecrow.

"That's right!" replied Sarah.

"He even told you about the still!" continued the Scarecrow.

"Yes!" answered Sarah.

"He even told you about getting drunk sometimes in the afternoon!' added the Scarecrow.

"Yes, he did!" said Sarah. "However, he wasn't proud of that."

"And he told you about the underground lake in the mine!" asked the Scarecrow.

"Well, no!" exclaimed Sarah. "What underground lake?"

"You didn't know about the underground lake? And you didn't know about the yellow streaks in the coal?" asked the Scarecrow.

"No!" stated Sarah. "He didn't tell me about an underground lake. And he didn't tell me about the yellow streak in the coal, because he didn't know about them!"

"No further questions at this time, Your Majesty!" said the Scarecrow. "However, I do reserve the right to recall the witness later."

"You may step down for now!" announced Ozma.

"What are you doing?" asked Walter of the Scarecrow.

"I am trying to create a reasonable doubt in the mind of Her Majesty!" replied the Scarecrow.

"I now want to address the issue of the method of the crime," stated the Woggle-Bug. "Here we have pictures of Joshua's body as it was found in the mine. In the picture the knife in his back and the hatchet in his head are quite noticeable. We wish to call this exhibit F."

"No objections!" called the Scarecrow.

"Next, I would like to introduce this knife and hatchet as the means that killed Joshua!" continued the Woggle-Bug. "These will be exhibits G and H."

"No objections!" replied the Scarecrow.

"I wish to recall the Wizard to the stand," announced the Woggle-Bug.

"Very well!" agreed Ozma. "Please remember Wizard that you are still under oath."

"Yes Your Majesty!" acknowledged the Wizard as he took the witness stand once more.

"Wizard, do you recognize this knife?" asked Dorothy.

"Yes, I do! It is the knife that I found stuck in Joshua's back," replied the Wizard. "Its tip had punctured his heart. That was at least one cause of his death."

"And did you notice any special markings on the knife?" inquired the Woggle-Bug.

"Why yes!" answered the Wizard. "If you look closely, you will find the initials W. F. craved on the handle of the knife."

"Wizard, do you recognize this hatchet?" questioned the Woggle-Bug.

"Yes, I do! It is the hatchet that I found buried in Joshua's head," responded the Wizard. "It caused severe bleeding in his split brain. That was the other cause of his death."

"And did you notice any special markings on the hatchet?" asked the Woggle-Bug.

"Why yes!" stated the Wizard. "If you look closely, you will find the engraved message -- Given to Benjamin Black by Joshua Smith.-- It is engraved at the base of the hatchet head."

"Your witness!" called the Woggle-Bug to the Scarecrow.

"Which killed Joshua, the knife or hatchet?" asked the Scarecrow.

"I cannot say!" replied the Wizard. "Given time, either wound would have been fatal."

"So, you cannot say for sure which weapon was actually the cause of Joshua's death," stated the Scarecrow.

"No, I can't!" agreed the Wizard.

"No further questions at this time," stated the Scarecrow. "However, I may wish to recall him later!"

"Very well," said Ozma. "You may step down for now!"

"I now recall Sarah Smith to the stand," requested the Woggle-Bug.

Sarah came to the stand. "I know," said Sarah, "I am still under oath!"

"Sarah, have you ever seen this knife and hatchet before?" asked the Woggle-Bug.

"Why yes!" acknowledged Sarah. "I have seen that knife on the belt of Walter Flounder. I helped Joshua decide what to engrave on that hatchet which Joshua gave to Benjamin Black."

"Will you take another look at the knife and hatchet?" requested the Woggle-Bug. The bailiff then gave the items to Sarah to look at.

"Yes, these are Walter's knife and Benjamin's hatchet!" stated Sarah once more.

"Your witness!" called the Woggle-Bug.

"I have no questions for her at this time," responded the Scarecrow. "Of course, I reserve the right to recall her later!"

"Very well, the witness can step down for now," announced Ozma.

"Now I want to address the issue of opportunity for committing the crime!" stated the Woggle-Bug. "We know that Joshua, Benjamin, and Walter all worked the mine together as partners. Who would have better access for burying Joshua in the mine? What better place to cover up the crime?"

"Are you making a speech, or do you have proof of that?" requested the Scarecrow.

"If you wish, we can recall Sarah and have her testify that Joshua, Benjamin, and Walter were partners," responded the Woggle-Bug. "They all work in the mine together, almost daily!"

The Scarecrow asked Benjamin and Walter about that. They said that it was public knowledge.

"Never mind!" answered the Scarecrow. "My clients admit that they were partners with Joshua, and that they worked the mine together."

"In that case, the Prosecution rests!" stated the Woggle-Bug.

"Very well, we will recess for lunch," announced Ozma. "Court will resume at two o'clock!"

Chapter 24
The Defense
Strikes Back

"Well? How are we doing?" asked Tommy.

"I think Professor Woggle-Bug did a good job of presenting the case!" replied Katie.

"But the trial is only getting started," commented Deborah. "Now we will find out how good their defense is."

The Woggle-Bug, Dorothy, and the Wizard joined Deborah, Katie, and Tommy for lunch. There was no more talk about the trial, even though they were all worried about it. It showed in their appetites. Everyone was counting the minutes until two o'clock.

Time passed slowly. Finally, two o'clock arrived.

"All rise! Court is now in session!" announced the Bailiff.

Her Majesty entered the room. "Please be seated," commanded Her Majesty, Ozma.

"Are you ready, Scarecrow and Tin Woodman?" asked Ozma.

"Yes Your Majesty!" replied the Scarecrow.

"In that case, let the Defense begin!" stated Ozma.

"First of all, my clients and I wish to agree with the prosecution on several points!" began the Scarecrow. "We admit that the knife and hatchet killed Joshua. We admit that the three of them were partners and worked the mine together. We admit the ownership of the knife and hatchet is as the prosecutor stated!"

After these remarks, the courtroom was stone quiet.

"In fact," continued the Scarecrow, "we only differ from the prosecution on two points! They are: 1) Benjamin and Walter are experienced miners and know that gold isn't found in a coal seam, and 2) that Joshua wasn't killed by them! Joshua died accidentally!"

"For my first witness," stated the Scarecrow, "I call Benjamin Black to the stand."

Benjamin Black got up and walked to the witness stand.

"Do you promise to tell the truth, the whole truth, and nothing but the truth?" asked the Bailiff.

"I do!" replied Benjamin.

"Please tell us in your own words how Joshua died!" requested the Scarecrow.

"It was all a terrible accident!" began Benjamin. "Joshua had been working on his moonshine still all day, and was in a state of intoxication by that afternoon. He heard someone coming and thought it might be the law. He jumped up from his work, knocking over a table, thus throwing a knife into the air. As he bent over in pain, the knife landed in his back. He stumbled around, tripped over the wood pile, and fell on the axe. When we found him in this state, we knew no one would believe the truth, so we buried him in the mine. Now we realize it was a dumb thing to do!"

"Are you and Walter experienced miners?" inquired the Scarecrow.

"Why, yes!" stated Benjamin. "Walter and I were miners in North Carolina for several years before we became partners with Joshua. We have worked in a gold mine and a precious stone mine."

"Your witness!" called the Scarecrow to the Woggle-Bug.

"Benjamin!" said Professor Woggle-Bug. "You said that you are an experienced miner. Is that Right?"

"Yes!" repeated Benjamin.

"Can you tell gold from sulfur?" asked the Woggle-Bug.

"Oh yes!' agreed Benjamin.

"Wizard!" requested the Woggle-Bug. "Would you mind showing Benjamin ore samples from exhibits C and E? Be careful to do it in such a way that Benjamin doesn't know which is which."

"One moment," replied the Wizard. He first went to the exhibit table. While keeping his body between him and Benjamin, he collected parts of the two exhibits. Her Majesty was able to watch everything.

On the bottom of each sample, he placed a tag telling which exhibit they were from. Next the Wizard picked up a sample in each hand. He showed each ore sample to Benjamin.

"Benjamin! Please tell us which hand holds which minerals," requested the Woggle-Bug.

The Wizard held out his two hands with the ore samples. Benjamin looked first at the right-hand sample and then at the left-hand sample.

"That's easy!" remarked Benjamin. "The sample in the Wizards right hand is sulfur crystals, such as we found in our coal mine. It is from exhibit C. The sample in the left hand is gold and must be from exhibit E."

"Are you sure that you got the exhibits correct?" asked Professor Woggle-Bug.

"Yes, I am!" stated Benjamin.

"Did he identify which sample was from which exhibit correctly?" inquired the Woggle-Bug of the Wizard.

"As the labels on the bottom of the samples will confirm, and as Her Majesty also witnessed, he did identify the samples sources correctly," answered the Wizard.

"You said that Joshua was killed in the afternoon!" stated the Woggle-Bug.

"Well, yes!" replied Benjamin. "Joshua worked a little in the mine in the morning. He joined us for lunch. I am sure that Sarah can tell you that Joshua ate the lunch she left for him. After lunch, he just worked on the still in the afternoon. That is, until his accident!"

"No more questions at this time," said the Woggle-Bug. "However, I do reserve the right to recall the witness later!"

"You may step down for now!" said Ozma.

"I wish to call one more witness," announced the Scarecrow. "This witness is willing to demonstrate how Joshua really died!"

"Objection!" cried the Woggle-Bug. "This trial is being held to determine that fact!"

"Sustained!" ruled Ozma. "Would you like to rephrase that statement?"

"This witness will show a possible way that Joshua could have died accidentally!" stated the Scarecrow. "I call Jack Pumpkinhead."

"Do you promise to tell the truth, the whole truth, and nothing but the truth?" asked the Bailiff.

"I do!" answered Jack.

"If the court will bear with me," requested the Scarecrow. "I will now set up a table, similar to the one Joshua had near his still. Here I am placing some objects and the knife from exhibit G. And over here I am building a small wood pile and placing the hatchet from exhibit H."

"Jack has brought a new head with him. His present one is worn out," continued the Scarecrow. "He will now use his old head, and his body stuffed with straw to demonstrate how Joshua might have died!"

Jack got up and walked over to the table by the pretend still. He then stooped down under the front of the table, but with him facing away from the table. Suddenly, he rose up, tripping over the table and throwing the knife into the air. As he bent back over, the knife landed in his back. Jack stumbled around for a few steps, and finally fell over backwards on the ground and wood pile. The ground drove the knife deep into his back, and his head landed on the edge of the hatchet.

Everyone in the courtroom was speechless at the results of the demonstration.

"Your witness!" called the Scarecrow.

"No questions, Your Majesty!" responded Professor Woggle-Bug.

"The defense rests!" stated the Scarecrow. He was proud of his good defense of his clients.

"Does the prosecutors have anything else to add?" asked Ozma.

"Yes Your Majesty!" replied Dorothy. "We wish to recall Sarah Smith to the stand!"

"Sarah, please take the stand again. Remember that you are still under oath!" cautioned Ozma.

Sarah retook the witness stand.

"Sarah!" requested the Woggle-Bug. "Did you see Joshua eat lunch with Benjamin and Walter on the day he disappeared?"

"No!" answered Sarah.

"Are you very sure?" asked the Woggle-Bug.

"I am very sure that I didn't see him eat lunch that day," stated Sarah.

"Your witness," called the Woggle-Bug to the Scarecrow.

Benjamin then had a short conference with the Scarecrow and the Tin Woodman.

"Sarah!" said the Scarecrow. "Did you prepare and bring a lunch to the mine for Joshua, Benjamin, and Walter on the day in question?"

"Yes, I did!" replied Sarah. "However, I didn't see any of them eat the lunch!"

"You did clean up after them?" asked the Scarecrow.

"Yes, I did!" answered Sarah.

"And what did you find when you cleaned things up?" inquired the Scarecrow.

"I found that all the food had been eaten!" stated Sarah.

"How many place settings had been used?" asked the Scarecrow.

"All three of the place settings had been used!" cried Sarah, even though she didn't want to say so.

"No more questions!" announced the Scarecrow.

"Sarah! What did you fix for their lunch?" requested the Woggle-Bug.

"I fixed sausage, bread, and carrots," replied Sarah.

"I wish to recall the Wizard as a witness," said Professor Woggle-Bug.

"Recall the Wizard," commanded Ozma. The Wizard took the witness stand.

"Wizard, did you do an autopsy on Joshua?" asked the Woggle-Bug.

"Yes, I did," replied the Wizard.

"And what did you find in his stomach?" requested the Woggle-Bug.

"I found some remains of fruit, eggs, and porridge!" answered the Wizard.

"No bread, sausage, or carrots?" questioned the Woggle-Bug.

"There was no bread, sausage, or carrots!" responded the Wizard.

"Based on this evidence, did Joshua eat that lunch?" asked Professor Woggle-Bug.

"No, he didn't," stated the Wizard.

"Wizard, would you tell the court what type ore you showed to Benjamin," requested the Woggle-Bug.

"The sample from exhibit C was crystallized sulfur," stated the Wizard.

"What was the sample from exhibit E?" asked the Woggle-Bug.

"That was fool's gold, otherwise known as iron pyrite!" answered the Wizard.

"That's not fair!" yelled Benjamin.

"Quiet in the court," commanded Ozma. "Scarecrow, please control your client!"

"I have no further questions," announced Professor Woggle-Bug.

"Neither do I have any more questions," added the Scarecrow.

"In that case, will the prosecution now give its closing argument," requested Ozma.

"Your Majesty!" began the Woggle-Bug. "The case is simple. Benjamin and Walter claim to have no motive, since they are experienced miners, but Benjamin can't tell fool's gold from real gold. They claim that Benjamin had lunch with them, and thus they didn't have the opportunity to kill Joshua, but the autopsy shows that Joshua didn't eat lunch. They admit to everything else. In short, Benjamin Black and Walter Flounder are guilty of murdering Joshua for his share of the mine which they thought contained gold."

"Will the defense now give its closing argument!" asked Ozma.

"Your Majesty!" said the Scarecrow. "I am happy to be before such a fair judge as you. Jack Pumpkinhead proved that it was possible for Joshua to have died accidentally! Joshua stomach didn't have any of lunch in it because he got drunk and threw up his lunch! The reason Benjamin didn't recognize the fool's gold, was because he was checking for the sulfur crystals. Once he did that, he didn't look very carefully at the other sample! There is more than a reasonable doubt that Joshua was murdered. It is even more doubtful that if Joshua was murdered that it was by Benjamin and Walter. It could have been some stranger trying to rob his still. Thank you!"

"Since both the prosecution and defense have presented their cases," announced Ozma, "court is recessed until ten o'clock tomorrow morning, at which time I will render my verdict!"

"All rise!" commanded the bailiff. Then, Her Majesty left the courtroom.

"Did we win or lose?" asked Tommy.

"We will find out tomorrow," answered Deborah. "For now, we just wait!"

Chapter 25
The Verdict
and Punishment

Everyone left the courtroom. Deborah and her friends had dinner together, visited a while, and finally went to bed. They had visions of how they thought the trial would end!

Joshua was still a ghost. He didn't sleep. So, he decided to visit Benjamin and Walter. Joshua first visited Benjamin's cell. Here he found Benjamin fast asleep. Benjamin looked like he didn't have a care in the world. Joshua started making haunting sounds. Benjamin just kept on sleeping. Then Joshua tried calling Benjamin's name.

"Bennnjaaammminnne, Bennnjaamminnne BBllaaaccckkk! I am here to hhhaaaaauuunnntt you!" said Joshua.

A sleepy Benjamin asked, "Who? What?".

"Benjamin!" called Joshua. "This is the ghost of Joshua Smith!"

Benjamin replied, "So what! You're dead. You killed yourself! So just go away." With that, Benjamin just turned over and went back to sleep.

"Well, that was a bust!" thought Joshua to himself. Then Joshua went to Walter's cell. Walter was not sleeping very soundly. He looked worried!

"Wwwaaallllttteerrr," haunted Joshua.

"Wwwhhaaaaattt wwaasss tthhaatt?" asked Walter, as he sat up in bed.

"Walter Flounder!" called Joshua, "I know you killed me for what you thought was gold! Now, I am going to haunt you for the rest of your life!"

"Oh no!" cried Walter. "Please, Joshua, anything but that!"

"It's too late, Walter!" continued Joshua.

"But I'll do anything!" pleaded Walter.

"You have only one chance!" replied Joshua. "You must confess your crime in court before the verdict is read! Otherwise, I will haunt you forever!"

"But they'll hang me!" complained a scared Walter.

"If you confess, you will not be hurt!" Joshua assured him. "I'll see to it that you don't even get any jail time!"

"Okay!" agreed Walter. "I'll confess, first thing at court tomorrow!"

"I'll be watching you!" warned Joshua. "Remember what you are going to do!" Finally, Joshua went back to his quarters.

Walter tried to go back to sleep. He finally decided that he would confess his crime tomorrow. Afterwards, Walter was able to sleep.

The next morning everyone got up, got dressed, and ate by themselves. Then they just wandered around the palace until ten o'clock. The courtroom was packed. Everyone wanted to know what the verdict would be.

The prosecutors and defenders were seated at their respective tables. Everyone was just waiting. Finally, the Bailiff announced, "Everyone please rise! The Royal Court of Oz is now in session." Her Majesty, Ozma, entered the courtroom and took her place.

"This court is now in session," called Ozma. "Please be seated!"

"Are the defendants ready to hear the verdict?" asked Ozma.

The Scarecrow, the Tin Woodman, Benjamin, and Walter all stood. "We are ready, Your Majesty!" replied the Scarecrow.

"In that case," began Ozma, "this Royal Court of Oz finds the defendants ...."

"One moment, Your Majesty," shouted Walter. "I wish to change my plea!"

The Scarecrow responded with a surprised, "What?"

The Tin Woodman had the same question.

Benjamin shouted, "What? Are you crazy? They have to find us not guilty after the Scarecrows great defense!"

"This is most irregular!" responded Ozma. "Please, let Walter finish what he has to say!"

"Your Majesty, I wish to plead guilty to murdering Joshua," stated Walter. "It is the only way I can get any peace!"

At this point, Benjamin grabbed Walter and started to strangle him. It was only the fast action of the Scarecrow, the Tin Woodman, and the Bailiff that saved Walters life.

Walter was barely able to breathe. When he was able to talk again, he said, "Everything the prosecution suggested about the crime was correct! We are guilty of murdering Joshua Smith."

The people in the courtroom all began talking excitedly at the same time. No one could hear what anyone else was saying.

"Order please! Order in the court!" commanded Ozma. "We will have order in the court or I will clear the courtroom! Will the defendants and all the counselors please see me in my quarters immediately?"

So, the Woggle-Bug, Dorothy, the Scarecrow, the Tin Woodman, Benjamin, and Walter all went to Ozma's quarters. No one was sure what to do next. Finally, Ozma asked, "Walter! Why are you doing this?"

"Because I am guilty and I haven't slept well since I helped kill Joshua!" replied Walter. "The ghost of Joshua said that I won't be killed or even have to go to jail if I would confess!"

"What?" exclaimed everyone at once.

"Bring the ghost of Joshua here! At once!" ordered Ozma. "Meanwhile, no one is to say anything!" A servant then ran out of Ozma's quarters and tried to carry out the order.

A few minutes later, two Oz Army officers escorted the ghost of Joshua into Ozma's quarters.

"Did you haunt Walter last night?" asked Ozma.

"Yes, I did," replied Joshua.

"How could you?" requested Ozma.

"Because that is what ghosts are supposed to do!" remarked Joshua. "I was only doing my duty!"

"Doing your DUTY!" exploded Ozma. "Did your duty include offering Walter no death or jail if he confessed?"

"Yes Your Majesty!' stated Joshua. "However, before we go any further, does Benjamin, also, wish to accept my offer?"

"If your offer is real, I will," replied Benjamin. "Then I can just write this whole thing off as a bad nightmare."

"But why?" questioned a puzzled Ozma.

"Because Oz can't jail or kill them without changing history!" answered Joshua. "And they aren't worth changing history over!"

"His right, Your Majesty!" replied Dorothy. "But I do have a punishment for them that will solve Joshua's problem. After all, that was the reason for our bringing everyone to Oz, wasn't it?"

"Well, yes!" agreed Ozma.

"Okay, then!" continued Dorothy. "Here is my proposal!" Dorothy then explained her idea to all that were present. Then everyone agreed to the terms and returned to the courtroom.

Once more, the Bailiff called the courtroom to order.

"I believe that we were listening to a change of a plea!" announced Ozma.

"Your Majesty!" stated the Scarecrow. "My clients wish to change their pleas to guilty!"

Suddenly the courtroom was very quiet.

"Furthermore," continued the Scarecrow. "In exchange for this, my clients wish to accept the punishment as suggested by the prosecutors!"

"And what is the punishment to be?" inquired Ozma.

"Your Majesty!" replied Dorothy. "Our only reason for holding this trial was to free the spirit of Joshua and allow him to find his eternal reward! We feel the following punishment will accomplish that goal. Therefore, this punishment will be sufficient for us!"

"And the punishment is?" asked Ozma.

"That first, each defendant will write a full confession explaining the crime!" explained Dorothy. "Second, each confession is to be placed in an envelope and be addressed to their ex-business partners, with an explanation on the envelope stating that it is to become part of their estates. Third, at the death of the last partner, the contents of the envelopes are to be published in the local newspaper. And fourth, that the heirs will keep the envelopes and contents forever. In place of forever, we will settle for two hundred years."

"Do the defendants agree to this?" asked Ozma.

"Yes, we do!" agreed Benjamin and Walter together. "We didn't profit from the crime at all, but we are suffering for what we did."

"You know," added Ozma, "that this will not guarantee any change in your eternal reward!"

"We will get what we deserve!" responded Benjamin and Walter.

"Very well!" announced Ozma. "The court accepts your change of plea and so orders that the before mentioned penalty be carried out! Court dismissed!"

Chapter 26
Deborah, Katie, and Tommy
Head for Home

Tommy, Katie, Deborah, the Scarecrow, the Tin Woodman, Glinda, the Wizard, the Woggle-Bug, Dorothy, Sarah, and Joshua were walking back to Dorothy's quarters after the trial.

"Wow!" remarked Tommy. "I didn't expect that ending for the trial!"

"Well, neither did I," agreed Katie.

"You will admit that the outcome of the trial was all that we could have hoped for," added Deborah.

"But what was the verdict that Her Majesty was about to announce?" asked Sarah. "What was it?"

"We will never know the answer to that question!" stated Dorothy. "However, Scarecrow, I must admit that you did give them one great defense. I hope I never again have to face off against you in court!"

"Yes!" agreed the Scarecrow. "I was very good even if I did surprise myself!"

"That seems to end Joshua's problems," remarked the Wizard. "As soon as the letters are prepared, all we need to do is get everyone back to their rightful place in time and space!"

"That will be Ozma's problem!" stated Dorothy. "Where are Benjamin and Walter?"

"Benjamin and Walter are under guard," replied the Scarecrow. "Her Majesty will see that they write the letters as quickly as possible. I would think they could easily finish them today!"

"Good!" exclaimed a joyful Joshua. "After that is accomplished, Sarah and I can go to our eternal reward! However, before we leave, I would like to ask a favor."

"And what might that be?" asked Dorothy.

"I would like to borrow that body again!" requested Joshua. "Just for the rest of the day. That way Sarah and I can say goodbye!"

"Sarah! If the suggestion is all right with you, then all you and Joshua need to do is go to his quarters. There, everything will be taken care of," Dorothy assured them.

"Oh, yes!" agreed Sarah. She and Joshua then ran back to Joshua's quarters.

"Well! Anyone interested in lunch?" asked the Wizard.

Suddenly everyone had their appetites back. So, all of them had lunch together at the Emerald City's fast food restaurant.

After lunch, Benjamin and Walter were brought before Ozma. Each of them showed her their letters. The letters were inspected and sealed with Her Majesty's own seal.

Once the seals were placed on the envelopes, Ozma agreed to send Benjamin and Walter back to their own time and place. First, Benjamin and Walter changed into the clothes which they were wearing when they first arrived in Oz. Finally, Ozma used her Magic Belt to place them back in their own time and place.

Deborah, Katie, Tommy, Rocky, Sigi, Dorothy, Glinda, the Wizard, the Scarecrow, and Jack Pumpkinhead were all invited to have dinner with Ozma. It seemed that Sarah and Joshua were busy elsewhere.

After dinner, everyone got a good night's sleep.

The next morning, Ozma sent Sarah back to her place in history, and Joshua gave up his temporary body. He was a ghost once again.

After having a good breakfast, Deborah, Katie, Tommy, Joshua the ghost, Rocky, and Sigi got ready to leave. Ozma lent them a carriage and the Sawhorse for the trip to the Nome Tunnel. She suggested that they visit the old Wicked Witch of the West's castle and Patchwork Village. These were in Winkie country. Dorothy and the Wizard went along for the ride.

The Wizard sat in the front seat with Katie and Tommy on each side of him. Dorothy sat in the back seat with Deborah on her left and Joshua on her right.

"Sawhorse," commanded the Wizard, "proceed at a safe speed to the old Wicked Witch of the West's castle. We want to be able to talk without fear of falling out of the carriage. Okay?"

"What? You mean you don't want to do any sightseeing?" replied a surprised Sawhorse. "In that case, just sit back and enjoy the ride. I'll get you to the castle by lunch time."

"Lunch time sounds like a good time to arrive," remarked Tommy. "Let us be off."

So, the Sawhorse set off at a moderate rate of speed. Soon they left the Emerald City behind, the grass and trees changed to a yellow hue.

"Why is everything yellow?" asked Joshua.

"Because we are now in Winkie Country," responded Katie. "The favorite color here is yellow."

"This country is ruled by the Tin Woodman," stated Dorothy, "and the Scarecrow also has his straw tower here."

"That's right," remarked Joshua, "we entered Oz at Winkie country, but it seems like that was years ago. So much has happened since then. Thank you for helping Sarah and I solve our problems."

Joshua and the others continued to talk about all their adventures for several hours. Time passed quickly. Before they realized it, the Sawhorse was announcing that the Wicked Witch's castle was just up ahead.

Everyone stopped talking and looked at the large castle coming into view.

"Wow!" remarked Dorothy. "That castle still looks large and menacing. This is where I accidentally killed the witch when she tried to take the silver shoes from me. She made me so mad that I threw a bucket of water at her. It was very frightening to watch the witch melt away. This place still gives me the creeps."

"So, there isn't any witch here anymore, is there?" asked Joshua.

"No, the witch is dead," replied Dorothy.

"That's good!" noted Tommy. "However Joshua, you are already a ghost, so the witch couldn't hurt you."

"Oh that's right!" recalled Joshua. "I forgot about that. Who lives there now?"

"I believe Ozma said the Winged Monkeys of Oz live there now," answered Deborah.

"No wonder," agreed Dorothy. "Most people don't want to live there after all the bad things that happened there during the Wicked Witch's rule."

"What are winged monkeys?" asked Katie.

"The winged monkeys are large monkeys that have wings and can fly," answered Dorothy. "Two winged monkeys can easily pickup and fly away with a person. On my first visit to Oz, the winged monkeys carried Toto, the Cowardly Lion, the Tin Woodman, the Scarecrow, and me off. At that time, they were controlled by the Wicked Witch. The Cowardly Lion, Toto, and I were flown to this castle. The monkeys tried to destroy the Scarecrow and the Tin Woodman.

Now that the winged monkeys are freed from the wicked witch's power, they are friendly. I am sure you will enjoy meeting them."

About this time, a winged monkey flew over the carriage. He then circled the carriage a few times. The Wizard asked the Sawhorse to stop the carriage. The winged monkey landed and approached the carriage.

"Your Highness," called the monkey to Dorothy, "what can we do for you?"

Dorothy answered, "I would like to show my friends the old Wicked Witch's castle. And I believe we would like to have lunch with your King."

"I am sure the King will be happy to grant you request," replied the monkey. "I'll let Him know you are coming." The monkey turned and flew away to the castle.

The Sawhorse started for the castle once more. Within a few minutes, he stopped the carriage at the main entrance to the castle. The King of the Winged Monkeys was at the entrance and greeted them.

"Your Highness, Princess Dorothy," greeted the King, "what a privilege to see you again. Won't you and your friends come inside and visit?"

"Thank you, Your Majesty," replied Dorothy. "We are honored to accept your invitation. May I introduce Deborah, Tommy, Katie, and Joshua the ghost to you?"

"It is always a pleasure to meet friends of Dorothy," stated the King.

"Hello Your Majesty," responded Deborah, Katie, Tommy, and Joshua, as they bowed to the King.

"Please come inside," said the King of the monkeys. "I would like to give you a tour of this castle and then invite you to lunch."

Everyone followed the King inside the castle. They received the grand tour. It included seeing the room where Dorothy had been held hostage and the courtyard where the Cowardly Lion was kept. Dorothy remarked on how much more cheerful the castle was now that the witch no longer ruled it. They toured the towers and the dungeons, and got to walk on the parapets.

"If you really like this castle," remarked the Monkey King, "then you should try seeing it from the air. If you like, I can have some of my winged monkeys carry you up high so you can see the whole castle at once."

Tommy and Katie accepted the Kings offer. The King had two monkeys each carry Tommy and Katie high up over the castle. It was a beautiful view. After Katie and Tommy landed, they told everyone about the wonderful view they had of Winkie Country.

After the tour, the King served a large lunch. Tommy, as always, enjoyed eating the lunch. Everyone enjoyed the meal except Joshua, who as a ghost couldn't eat. Joshua enjoyed talking to the King while the others ate. He was the first ghost that the King had seen. All the winged monkeys enjoyed meeting Joshua.

Once lunch was completed, Dorothy and her party said farewell to the King of the monkeys, got back into their carriage and continued their journey.

Chapter 27
A Short Visit to the
Patchwork Village

The party rode along in silence for the first hour after lunch. Everyone was full from lunch and didn't feel like talking. Before they knew it, the Sawhorse announced that the Patchwork Village was just up ahead.

"What is the Patchwork Village?" asked Katie.

"That's a good question!" agreed Tommy. "It wouldn't be where the repair-people live that do all the repair work in Oz?"

"I believe that Ozma said it is where Scraps, the Patchwork Girl of Oz lives when she isn't staying in the Emerald City," replied Dorothy, "but I have never been there myself."

"So, this will be a new experience for all of us," announced Deborah, "that is unless the Wizard has been here before."

"Well no, I haven't been here before either," answered the Wizard, "so yes, this will be a new experience for all of us."

The Sawhorse pulled the carriage down the main street of Patchwork Village and stopped at the steps of the city hall. The Mayor of the Patchwork Village came out to greet them. His clothes were all covered with colorful patches.

"Welcome, Princess Dorothy and friends, to the Patchwork Village," greeted the Mayor. "How may we help you?"

"We would like to see and learn a little about the Patchwork Village," stated Dorothy, "and may I introduce my friends, the Wizard of Oz, Deborah, Katie, Tommy, and Joshua."

"Well, it is a pleasure to meet all of you," responded the Mayor. "I am very glad to get to see Joshua the ghost. We have heard so much about him. He does look so scary.

"The Patchwork Village was built and named in honor of Scraps, the Patchwork Girl of Oz," continued the Mayor. "As you can see, all the citizens of the Patchwork Village wear many colorful patches on their clothes in her honor. Scraps stays here from time to time, and is our most honored citizen. I believe she is here today!"

"Can we meet her?" asked Katie. "I have never seen a live patchwork doll."

"I will send a messenger at once to see if she will see you," declared the Mayor. "She came here last night. It seems the Emerald City is tired of all her whimsy once more. The Patchwork Girl is welcome here for a few days until the Emerald City folks miss her once more. At that time she will be invited back to the palace in the Emerald City."

"I should warn you," continued the Mayor, "Scraps is a life size patchwork doll. Not only is she alive, but most of the time, she talks in rhythms. She is also a fun loving character that can get on ones nerves."

'So, this could be called Scraps' hideout when she causes too much trouble," remarked Tommy.

"You could say that," agreed the Mayor, "but Scraps can't help what she is. She was made from a patchwork quilt by Margolotte, the wife of Dr. Pipt. The Patchwork Girl was brought to life by Dr. Pipt, the Crooked Magician. Ojo, a Munchkin boy, accidentally got too much cleverness powder in Scraps' brain. Therefore, at times, Scraps can be hard to get along with, but she means no harm."

About that time, a messenger returned and told the Mayor that Scraps would be right out. Shortly thereafter, Scraps arrived.

"Howdy--do?" greeted Scraps, and then she started talking in rhythms.

"I'm the Patchwork Girl that's come to life;
I'm as whimsical and fun loving as they come;
Welcome, one and all!"

"Hello," responded everyone, as they stared at Scraps colorful outfit.

"I really like the fellow," continued Scraps;

"That hasn't got a body.

"What a nice decoration you have on your head!"

"I am afraid the hatchet was part of what killed me," stated Joshua. "If you take a good look at my back, you will see a knife sticking out of it."

"Oh dear!" remarked Scraps.

"You have a knife and a hatchet sticking out of you;

You are my first ghost and I declare;

For a human, you look terrible!"

"Well ghosts are known for scaring people," stated Joshua, "but enough about me. Won't you show us around your village?"

"I would be most honored to show you around the Patchwork Village," answered Scraps, the Patchwork Girl. "Why don't you just follow the Mayor and me?"

So, everyone got a tour of the Patchwork Village. All the inhabitants of the village dressed as if their clothes came from patchwork quilts. The drapes, the rugs, and anything else that was made from cloth, was covered with colorful patches. It was a very colorful tour!

The tour included a large community sewing room. It was full of persons sewing colorful patches on everything imaginable. Most of these items were to be placed in the Patchwork Village shops.

The tour ended at the city hall. Next, Deborah, Katie, Tommy, and Joshua were allowed to visit the shops on villages' main street. If there was anyway to place cloth on an item, then the shops sold that item with patchwork all over it. One could buy a patchwork tent, patchwork covered canteens, and patchwork backpacks. There were clothes of all descriptions. This was one place in Winkie Country where yellow was not a favorite color!

Tommy decided to buy himself a new flashlight whose handle was covered in patchwork material. Katie bought herself a new patchwork covered purse. Deborah purchased herself some nice patchwork handkerchiefs and a new patchwork covered hat. She would need a new hat to replace the one ruined in the mine.

"We want to thank you for the tour of Patchwork Village," stated Dorothy. "It is a most beautiful village."

"Well, we want to thank you for a chance to see Joshua the Ghost!" responded Scraps. "I am glad that everything worked out well for Joshua. Is he soon to cease being a ghost?"

"Why yes," answered Deborah. "Joshua, Tommy, Katie, and I are on our way home now. Once we get safely home, Joshua should get released to his eternal reward."

"Thanks again for the visit," commented Scraps. "I only wish we could have seen Sarah as a ghost as well."

"Sarah has already been sent home," stated Dorothy. "I am sure she will also shortly be going to her eternal reward." With that, the group walked back to the carriage.

Everyone got back into the carriage. They waved goodbye to Scraps, the Patchwork Girl of Oz, and the Mayor and citizens of the Patchwork Village. The Wizard had the Sawhorse continue on to the Nome tunnel. It took another hour of traveling to reach the tunnel.

Joshua, Tommy, Katie, and Deborah said goodbye to the Sawhorse, the Wizard, and Dorothy. Everyone thanked everyone else for the pleasure of their company on the trip. Joshua was very grateful for all the help he received from the Land of Oz.

At the tunnel, they switched to motorized carts driven by nomes for the trip back to the lost coal mine.

They traveled through the Nome Tunnel to the Land of the Nome King. Here they visited the guest quarters for long enough to change back into the clothes they wore for the hike. They had not been cleaned! Katie complained about having to wear the dirty clothes. Deborah remained her that they won't be in clean clothes after two days in a coal mine.

Then they took a cart back to the tunnel that led back to the lost coal mine. They came out of this tunnel by the volcano at the underground lake.

"Oh no!" thought Deborah, aloud. "We are going to have to crawl back through that hole to get to the mines tunnel."

A nome had Tommy get out of the cart and took him over to an old river bed. He pointed at a stone and told Tommy to pick it up and say nothing. Tommy picked up the stone and put it in his pocket. It just looked like a dirty lump of glass to Tommy.

Next, the nome and Tommy got back into the cart. Much to Deborah's relieve, the cart reentered the tunnel. It went a short distance and turned into another tunnel. This tunnel ended at the lost coal mine by the tunnel next to the hole leading to the lake.

Deborah, Katie, Tommy, Joshua, Rocky, and Sigi got out of the cart. The nomes informed Deborah and the others that they had been returned to the mine on the night of the full-moon. Well even stranger things were possible when dealing with the Land of Oz. The group started the long dusty walk back to the cave-in.

The nomes moved the cart back into their tunnel. Finally, they filled in their tunnel entrance so well that no one could see it had ever existed. Now all Deborah, Katie, Tommy, Sigi, and Rocky had to do was wait to be rescued.

Chapter 28
George Goes
Searching for Them

George got off work a few minutes after five o'clock. He climbed into his car and drove over to Deborah's house. He arrived at Deborah's house at five twenty-five. No one was home. George thought nothing of it; after all he was a little early. He waited in his car. Time passed. George waited some more. Finally, about six o'clock, George began to get concerned. It wasn't like Deborah to be this late.

He called Tammy, his wife, on his cellular phone. "Hello, Tammy!" greeted George. "Have you heard from Deborah, since I dropped off Katie and Tommy?"

"Why no!" responded Tammy. "Aren't you supposed to pick them up after work?"

"I'm at Deborah's house now," replied George, "but there isn't anyone home. I thought perhaps there might have been a change of plans?"

"No!" answered Tammy. "I have heard nothing from Katie, Tommy, or Deborah. Should I be worried?"

"Now don't get upset!" cautioned George. "I am sure it is nothing. Maybe they just lost track of time. Or maybe they had car trouble. I'll just go look for them. Okay?"

"If you think that is best, George" replied Tammy. "Let me know if you find out anything."

"Okay! I will!" George assured her. "I'll call you later. Goodbye!"

"Very well!" agreed a concerned Tammy. "Goodbye!"

George put away his cellular telephone and went looking for them. When he reached the turn-off for Pothole Creek, he found a police roadblock.

When George asked the police if he could go to Opossum Bottom, he was told the road was closed. There had been a flash flood. The road wasn't safe. George told the police that his two children and aunt had gone for a hike up Opossum Bottom Hollow and hadn't returned. The police told him to go to the police station and file a missing persons report. Then the search and rescue person in the area would be told to look out for them.

A discouraged George went to the police station and filled the report. He was then told to go home. The police would contact him.

George went home and told Tammy what had happened. Tammy said the news had mentioned some flash floods but didn't give any details. Tammy and George spent a long night waiting for the telephone to ring. Finally they went to bed.

The next morning, Tammy insisted that George go to work. She would call if there was any news.

George went to work. It was a very long day for him. Finally work was over. George went home. Tammy had no news for him. He called the police on his cell phone. They had no news. George ate a quick dinner. He then told Tammy he was going looking for the children and auntie. He placed some hiking equipment in the car and left.

When he got to the Pothole Creek turn-off, it was open. He was able to drive all the way to the Opossum Bottom Trading Post.

He found Deborah's car at the Opossum Bottom Trading Post. He asked the manager about the car and found out they were there the morning before last, and the manager hadn't seen them since. They said they were going hiking.

It is dark when George started hiking up the Opossum Bottom canyon. There had been a large amount of water through the canyon floor. While no homes were damaged, the paved road in the floor of the canyon was all broken up. He took a large lantern, a compass, and his cellular phone with him. There was a full-moon. George saw the marks left by the high waters the day before during the flash flood. He walked along the high-level water mark on the trading post side of the canyon. He looked for any sign that Dorothy, Katie and Tommy had been by where he was. George spent two hours or so covering three to four miles. He was tired and ready to give up for the night. Upon the hill side on his left, he noticed the moon light striking some white, rectangular rocks. He decided to investigate the rocks before giving up for the night.

George found the graveyard, but found no foot prints because of the earlier heavy rains. While he was looking at the grave marker for Sarah, his light reflected off something shiny on the ground. He kicked the object loose with his foot.

He had uncovered the foil inner wrapper and outer wrapper of a Big Willies Peanut-butter and Jelly Bar. George continued looking around. Next, he found an empty box of Malt Flavored Chocolate Balls. George now knew that Tommy and Katie had been here before or during the heavy rain storm.

George got out his cellular phone and called the Sheriffs office.

"Sheriffs Office!" answered a Deputy. "What can I do for you?"

George stated, "This is George Gilbert. I need help in finding three lost hikers. My children and their Aunt Deborah went hiking up Opossum Bottoms canyon, yesterday morning. There was a flash flood through this area at noon yesterday. I have found signs that they were here at the lost graveyard."

"Did you say the lost graveyard?" asked the Deputy.

"Yes!" answered George. "It is three or four miles up the canyon beyond Opossum Bottoms Hollow. I am there now! The road is all broken up from the flash flood. You will need a four-wheel drive vehicle to reach here."

The Deputy Sheriff responded, "Stay where you are! We will get a man out to you in about thirty minutes."

Twenty-five minutes later, George could see lights from a vehicle coming up the canyon toward him. He worked his way down the hillside to the valley below.

As the vehicle got closer, George started waving his lantern back and fourth. The driver of the vehicle saw the light and flashed the vehicles headlights on and off. George then waited for the vehicle to reach him.

"Hello!" greeted the driver of the vehicle. "I am Deputy Sheriff Jones. Are you George Gilbert?"

"Yes, I am!" replied George. "I am glad to see you folks!"

"You said that you found signs of your missing children and Aunt at the lost graveyard?" stated the Deputy.

"Yes, I did!" agreed George. "The graveyard is up the hillside. If you follow me, I'll take you there."

"Well, if this is really the lost graveyard," remarked the Deputy, "then there are a lot of folks that would like to know about it. Please! Lead the way."

So, George and the Deputy worked their way up the hillside to the lost graveyard. This took them several minutes.

"Well I'll be!" exclaimed the Deputy. "It does look like you found the lost graveyard. And look! There's the statue of Sarah what's her name. Did you know that the statues head is supposed to turn sometimes and point to a lost gold mine?"

"I have heard some of those stories," commented George. "Of course I didn't place much faith in them. Oh goodness! I don't believe it!"

"Now what?" requested the Deputy.

"When I looked at the statue earlier," recalled George, "the head was pointed straight ahead. Now look at it. It seems to be looking over its left shoulder!"

"So, it does!" admitted the Deputy. "And this just happens to be a night with a full-moon!"

"Well, if you will just look at the moon for yourself," suggested George. "Also, I know the head has moved since I first looked at it!"

"Okay!" replied the Deputy. "Let's assume you're right, and not just seeing things because you are tired! What should we do next?"

'I'm not sure!" responded George. "Maybe we should go looking in the direction that the head is pointing."

"Sure! Why not?" agreed the Deputy. "It looks like the head is pointing up the hill in that direction, up toward those bushes."

"Well, that isn't very far!" stated George. "It won't take long to check it out, not more than a minute or two. Surely, that isn't asking too much?"

"Lead on!" agreed the reluctant Deputy. So, George and the deputy walked up the hill to the bushes. George moved aside several bushes. His lantern then picked up the old mine sign.

"What do you make of this, Deputy?" asked George.

"I'll be a blue nosed roof rat! It says BLACK HOLE GOLD MINE!" answered the deputy. "I wonder where the mine shaft is."

"I bet it's over there behind those other bushes," suggested George.

George and the Deputy went over to the bushes and looked behind them. They found the entrance to the mine.

"I do believe my light is showing some tracks in the dust!" remarked George.

The Deputy looked at the ground in the mine shaft. There he saw people and animal tracks.

"You are right about the tracks!" announced the Deputy. "There seems to be a medium size foot print, one or two smaller foot prints, and the tracks of an animal or two. Looks like your party went into the mine."

"The tracks could belong to my Aunt, my children, and my Aunts dog Sigi!" replied George. "Perhaps we should take a quick look inside?"

"I don't like old mine shafts!" responded the Deputy. "They can be dangerous. Maybe, if we are very careful, we can follow the tracks for a little ways."

George and the deputy cautiously entered the mine, following the tracks in the dust.

Chapter 29
George and the Sheriff Find Deborah and Others

Deborah, Katie, Tommy, Rocky, and Sigi had just walked back up to the cave-in of the lost coal mine. Now, they had to wait for George to find them. Meanwhile, the nomes had left and had filled in the tunnel they used for taking the group to Oz and back. No trace was left to show that the nomes had ever been there.

"Tommy," requested Deborah, "I think you should turn on your walkie-talkie. Your father may remember that you have it with you. He might try to contact you on it."

"I forgot all about the walkie-talkies," remarked Tommy, as he reached up to his helmet and switched on the walkie-talkie.

"Okay, kids," said Deborah, "we need to get our story ready for your father. You know he will never believe you went to Oz."

"Right!" replied Katie. "I don't think he believes in Oz. So, let me see if I have things straight? We are back, trapped in the mine, and it is the night of the day after our hike. Is that right?"

"That's right," agreed Deborah. "We have been trapped for a day and a half. That is long enough so that we would be good and scared!"

"And we would have run down some of our flashlight batteries!" added Tommy. "Did we find the underground lake?"

"Yeah!" asked Katie as well. "That is a good question."

"Yes, we found the lake!" stated Deborah. "We also found that there was no way out at the lake, so we came back to here. Okay!"

"Yes!" replied Tommy and Katie.

"Arf!" replied Sigi.

"Hisss!" replied Rocky.

"Well, we must be back in the outside world," commented Tommy.

"You are right, brother!" added Katie. "The animals can no longer talk like us!'

"By my watch," said Deborah, "it is about midnight. So, we have been in the mine for about a day and a half. That gives us enough time for our exploration of the mine and lake."

Meanwhile, the Sheriffs Deputy and George were walking slowly down the main tunnel of the mine. They were following the tracks left by Deborah, Katie, Tommy, Rocky, and Sigi.

"You are right, Mr. Gilbert," said the Deputy. "These are fresh tracks. It does look like they may have come in here to get away from the storm. However, I still don't know how they managed to find this mine!"

"Sheriff!" said George. "Do you have a citizens band walkie-talkie with you?"

"Why?" asked the Deputy.

"Because my kids have handless walkie-talkies with them!" replied George. "They are set for band D. Maybe they can be contacted by radio?"

"Well, it is worth a try!" replied the Deputy. So he took out the walkie-talkie, made some adjustments to it and gave a call on it.

"This is the Sheriffs Department to Deborah, Katie, or Tommy," said the deputy. Next, he listened for a couple of minutes. At first he heard nothing but static, then the walkie-talkie became silent.

"I don't know how far the radio will carry in this mine," stated George. "Perhaps we should go further down the tunnel?"

"It should be okay as long as we see only one set of tracks!" replied the Deputy. "That way we can just follow them in the other direction to get back out of here!"

Meanwhile, Deborah and friends are trapped in the mine, listening to their walkie-talkie.

"Auntie!" announced Tommy. "I just heard several seconds of static on the walkie-talkie."

"Well, try answering them," suggested Deborah. "Maybe they can hear you."

So, Tommy tried sending on his walkie-talkie. After which, he listened for a minute or two. "There doesn't seem to be anything else on the walkie-talkie," replied Tommy.

"Well, just keep listening!" said Deborah.

Back with George and the Deputy, things were moving slowly.

"Okay," said the Deputy. "We will follow these tracks for a while." So, George and the Deputy followed the tracks down the tunnel. Shortly, they came to the left turn in the main tunnel.

"I am sure this turn in the tunnel isn't helping the walkie-talkies," remarked George. "After we make the turn, why don't you try talking on the walkie-talkie again?" George and the Deputy turned the corner of the tunnel and continued down it.

"Deborah, Tommy, or Katie, this is the Sheriffs Department!" said the Deputy. "Can you hear me?"

"Hello!" said Tommy into the walkie-talkie. "Does anyone hear me? I think I hear your signal. If you hear me, please click your transmitter on and off, twice."

"Brother, you heard something?" asked Katie.

"Quiet!" demanded Tommy, being careful to cover his microphone with his hand. Tommy listened carefully for a moment or two. Finally, he heard the noise come and go twice on his receiver.

"I got someone on the walkie-talkie!" cried an excited Tommy. "But I can't understand them. However, they can understand me!"

"Well, tell them to come further down the tunnel," said Deborah. "When they get closer, we should be able to understand them."

"This is Tommy Gilbert," spoke Tommy into the walkie-talkie. "I still can't understand you. We are trapped in the mine! Maybe if you come closer then I may be able to understand you!"

"George," stated the Deputy, "I have a Tommy Gilbert on the walkie-talkie, but he can't understand us. He says they are trapped in the mine. Maybe if we get closer to them, he will be able to understand us?"

"I think we need to keep following their tracks," agreed George. "Thank goodness they seem to be all right!"

So, George and the Deputy kept following the tracks. They went right past the first tunnel on the left without even stopping. Since the tracks didn't go that way, they didn't bother with that tunnel. Soon they came to the place where the main tunnel split into three tunnels. Here the tracks went to the tunnel on the right. George and the Deputy went down the tunnel on the right.

"Why don't you try the walkie-talkie again?" suggested George.

"Sure thing," replied the Deputy. "This is the Sheriffs Department, can you hear me?"

"This is Tommy Gilbert?" replied Tommy. "Did you say that you are the Sheriffs Department?"

"Tommy can hear me," reported the Deputy, to George. "What do we do now?"

"Tell them that I am with you," said George. "Next, ask them where they are?"

"Tommy!" called the Deputy. "I am a deputy sheriff and I have George Gilbert with me. Where are you?"

"Auntie!" said Tommy. "They can hear us, and Dad is with them!"

"Tell them that the three of us are all right," requested Deborah.

"Deputy!" radioed Tommy. "Auntie, Katie, Sigi, and I are all right. We are trapped by a cave-in, a little ways down the tunnel on the right of three tunnels."

"Tommy says they are all right!" said the Deputy. "They are trapped by a cave-in just down this tunnel a little ways."

About this time, George and Deputy came upon the cave-in.

"Tell them we have found the cave-in," said George. "It looks like we are going to need some picks and shovels."

"Tommy," called the Deputy, "We have found the cave-in. We will have to go back and get some pick and shovels. We'll be back shortly."

"Okay!" answered Tommy. "We're not going anywhere!"

"Auntie," said Tommy. "They have found the cave-in. Now they need to go back to get some tools."

"Great!" cried a happy Katie. "So now we just have to wait!"

"I suggest you try sleeping," said Deborah. "It could take them awhile."

So Deborah, Katie, and Tommy tried to rest while they waited to be rescued.

Meanwhile George and the Deputy went back out to the Deputy's four-wheel drive vehicle. "Sheriffs Office," said the Deputy, into his car radio, "This is Deputy Jones. I have found George Gilbert. We then found the missing hikers trapped in the lost coal mine. Can you send us some picks and shovels, and maybe a wheel barrow?"

"This is the Sheriffs Office!" replied a voice over the radio. "We have a search and rescue team on the way to you. They have the equipment you requested. Did you say a lost coal mine?"

"Thank you!" said the Deputy. "And yes we found the lost mine that goes with the lost graveyard. I'll tell you more at a later time. This is Deputy Jones out!"

George and the Deputy only had a short wait for the search and rescue team. First they saw the lights of the search and rescue vehicle about one-half mile away. Within several minutes, the vehicle had drawn up next to the Deputy's vehicle. There was a man and a woman in the vehicle.

"Hello!" said the man who was the driver of the vehicle. "We were told that some people are missing."

"Not anymore," replied the Deputy. "We've found them, trapped by a cave-in about one-fourth of a mile into that old mine." The Deputy was pointing up the hillside, beyond the graveyard.

"I didn't know there were any mines out here!" stated the woman. "By the way, I am Judy and this is Don."

"Hello, Judy and Don!" replied George. "This is Deputy Jones and I am George Gilbert. The three missing persons are my Aunt Deborah and my children, Katie and Tommy. They are trapped in the old lost coal mine that has been a legend around here for many years. The legend also includes a lost graveyard. It is up next to the mine."

"I thought that was a lost gold mine!" stated Don.

"Well, it was supposed to have been a gold mine," agreed George, "but around these parts, the most valuable thing one is going to find is coal. The mine is black with coal."

"Let me get this right!" said Judy. "You say they are trapped. What do we need to get to them out?"

"How do you know that they are trapped in that mine?" asked Don. "Do you know if they are hurt?"

"We talked to them on a walkie-talkie," replied the Deputy. "They are fine. However, we need to dig out a caved-in section of the tunnel. I think some picks and shovels will do the task!"

"Well, we have two shovels and a pick with us," replied Judy. "Don and I will get the shovels and pick. Can you help carry some portable lights?"

"Sure thing," replied George. So, Judy gave one portable light each to George and the Deputy. Judy picked up the pick and Don grabbed the two shovels. The group headed for the mine. It took about ten minutes for them to reach the cave-in.

"Tommy!" called the Deputy into the walkie-talkie. "We are back with the tools. Just sit tight and we will dig you out."

"This is Katie," replied Katie into her walkie-talkie. "It is nice to hear from you again. We have nothing else to do, so we will just sit here and wait for you."

"Help has arrived!' exclaimed Deborah.

"Good!" remarked Tommy. "I am getting tired of this mine!"

"They're still okay," said the Deputy to the others.

George and the Deputy set up the portable lights. Don and Judy put down the shovels and pick and took a look at the cave-in. Don climbed up the pile of rocks and used a flashlight to look between the tunnel roof and the pile of rocks.

"This roof looks stable," stated Don. "I think all we need to do is remove the top of this pile. After that is done, we should be able to see the tunnel on the other side."

So Don started working with the pick where the pile of rocks went past the tunnel roof. George and the Deputy used the shovels to remove the rocks that Don knocked lose. These rocks were spread out along the sides of the tunnel. Judy kept moving the portable lights around so everyone could see what they were doing. It took about five minutes to remove enough rocks so that Don could get between the tunnel roof and the pile of rocks.

"We're in luck!' called Don. "The cave-in is only a few feet wide up here at roof level. It should only take a few minutes to clear a path to the tunnel roof on the far side of the cave-in. After that, I may be able to knock the rocks down the far side of the cave-in."

"Deputy!" said George. "I think you should tell Tommy or Katie what is going on. Perhaps you should have them move back away from the cave-in area."

"That's a good idea!" replied the Deputy. He spoke into the walkie-talkie. "Katie or Tommy, we have gotten to the top of the cave-in. You should move back down the tunnel a little ways, so we can try pushing rocks down your side of the cave-in."

"This is Katie!" answered Katie into her walkie-talkie. "We are moving back down the tunnel about fifty feet. Will that do?"

"That will be fine," replied the Deputy. "Okay, Don! They are out of the way. See what you can do with the pick."

Don started loosening rocks from the pile by the tunnel roof on the far side of the slide. It only took a few tries before he had made a hole big enough for him to get through.

About this time, Sigi ran up the pile of rocks, through the hole, across the top of the pile and down the other side to George.

"Arf! Arf!" barked a happy Sigi.

"Well, now! Who have we here?" asked Judy.

"This is Sigi," said George. "He is Aunt Deborah's dog. How are you doing Sigi?"

Sigi just barked hello some more.

"Hello!" said Don. "Can you folks hear me?"

"We hear you and see you," called Tommy.

"We sure are glad to see you," yelled Katie.

"Welcome to the Black Hole Gold Mine," announced Deborah, as they all walked up to the cave-in pile of rocks.

"Let me make this hole a little larger," said Don. "Then, you can all climb through it, that is, if you are ready to leave this mine?"

"We're ready," they all replied together.

So Don took a minute or two to enlarge the hole. Finally, Deborah, Katie, Tommy, Sigi, and Rocky could climb out of the blocked tunnel.

Katie went first. She handed Don her backpack before she tried to get through the hole. It was easy for her. Deborah followed Katie. Deborah worked a little harder at getting through the hole, but made it without any major problems. Next Tommy got Rocky the raccoon to go through the hole. Lastly, Tommy climbed through the hole.

"Daddy!" cried Katie and Tommy and ran up to George. "We are glad to see you!" They threw their arms around him. George was very glad to see them as well.

Rocky headed straight for Sigi. He was scared by being with all these people.

"What's with the raccoon?" asked George.

"Oh that's Rocky," remarked Tommy.

"He is the one who showed us where the lost mine was hidden," said Katie.

"Do we have a story for you!" commented Deborah. "However, first I think we should get out of this mine before anything else happens to us. Once we are out of here, we will tell you what happened to us. Okay?"

"I think that's a good idea," agreed Judy. Everyone gathered up their equipment and started walking toward the mine entrance. It only took five minutes or so before they were all out of the mine.

Rocky stopped at the mine entrance. He hissed goodbye to Sigi and then ran back into the mine. Sigi replied with an, "Arf!"

"Well, I guess Rocky has had enough of our company," stated Deborah. "I am sure he can take better care of himself than we could. So long Rocky. It was nice to have met you!"

"So long, Rocky!" called Tommy and Katie together.

"Now just how did you managed to get trapped in that old mine tunnel?" asked George.

"Well, we went for a hike up this canyon," began Deborah.

"Next we had lunch down there by the creek," added Tommy.

"And Tommy saw the stones of the lost graveyard when the wind blew the bushes about," said Katie.

"So we climbed up to look at the graveyard," continued Deborah.

"While we were looking at it that bad storm hit," recalled Tommy.

"And Sigi chased Rocky into the hidden lost mine," stated Katie.

"We took cover from the storm in the mine entrance," added Deborah.

"Sigi chased Rocky down the mine tunnel," said Tommy.

"Next, Tommy chased after Sigi," remembered Katie.

"And we had to go find Tommy," explained Deborah.

"Then, the roof fell in," related Katie.

"And we looked for another way out," told Tommy.

"And we found an underground lake, and fell down a water fall," added Katie.

"And the ghost of Joshua Smith tried to haunt us," stated Deborah. "He claims he was murdered and buried at the end of the first tunnel on the left."

"Of course that happened about two-hundred years ago," said Tommy.

"And that about covers our story," finished Deborah.

"I think we should take these folks home for now," suggested the Deputy. "I can get a statement from them tomorrow. What do you think?" To himself, the Deputy was thinking, "What a strange story."

"I think it has been a long day," replied George. "Let's go home!"

"A ghost indeed," he muttered as he climbed into his car. "They were in the mine too long a time."

So, everyone got into the vehicles and started home. On the way, the Deputy reported on his radio that the lost people had been found and everyone was okay.

The vehicles stopped at the Opossum Bottoms Trading Post, where Deborah and Sigi got in her car, and George, Katie and Tommy got in their car. Everyone said goodbye to everyone else and they all went home.

Chapter 30
Joshua's Murder Solved

Late Wednesday morning, the Sheriff picked up Deborah and drove her over to the home of Katie and Tommy. The Sheriff and Deborah went into the living room, where Tammy was waiting with Katie and Tommy.

"First of all, I want to congratulate you on surviving the flash flood and the mine cave-in!" stated the Sheriff. "Not many folks can say they survived such disasters!"

"Okay, folks!" continued the Sheriff. "I am here to listen to your story of how you found the lost mine. You can also tell me what you think you know about Joshua Smith and his possible murder. Afterwards, I will decide what should be done next."

"Well, we first found the lost graveyard when we were having lunch on our hike," began Deborah. "Tommy saw some square stones when the wind blew the bushes around just right."

"So, we walked up to the stones to see what they were," continued Tommy. "There we found the graveyard. While we were looking around, we found the statue of Sarah Smith. Auntie said that it was the lost graveyard mentioned in legends about this area."

"While we were looking at the grave markers," contributed Katie, "the big storm sneaked up on us. We were deciding what to do, when Sigi chased the raccoon into the lost mine. Tommy followed Sigi and found the mine entrance. Next, we took cover in the mine entrance."

"We intended to just wait out the storm at the mine entrance!" told Deborah. "However, before I knew it, Sigi started chasing the raccoon down the mine tunnel. And Tommy ran after Sigi."

"That was dumb of me!" announced Tommy. "I guess I wasn't thinking. I only wanted to get Sigi back. Before I knew it, I was a long way down the tunnel, just past where the cave-in was located."

"Of course, it hadn't caved-in yet," remarked Katie. "Anyway, Auntie and I went after Tommy. Fortunately by this time, Tommy and Sigi stopped moving. After a while we were able to track Tommy to where he and Sigi were waiting."

"Just as we were going to come back to the entrance of the mine, the roof fell in!" explained Deborah. "So, we had to look for another way out. If you go to the far end of the tunnel where we had the cave-in, you will find a hole that leads to the underground lake. It also has some small volcano activities."

"While we were trying to get down to the lake, we fell down a waterfall," commented Tommy. "Next, we had dinner by the hot water pool near the volcano and stayed there overnight. There was an old river bed near it where I found this dirty piece of glass." Tommy held up the rock the nome had given him. He had forgotten about it until now.

"And finally, we made our way back to the cave-in," added Katie, "where we went to sleep and were awakened by Tommy hearing you on the radio!"

"Oh! While we were waiting to be rescued, we were visited by the ghost of Joshua Smith," remarked Deborah. "At least that's what he said his name was."

"He said he had been murdered a long time ago!" recalled Tommy. "And his body is buried at the end of the first tunnel on the left."

"Oh, and it was his ex-business partners, Benjamin Black and Walter Flounder that murdered him!" stated Katie.

"He was murdered for what his partners thought was gold in a coal seam," continued Tommy. "They didn't want to share the wealth with Joshua."

"But the gold turned out to be sulfur deposits in the coal," finished Katie.

"And before you ask!" added Deborah. "No! We are not confused! We didn't use to believe in ghosts. However, if this was a dream, then we all had the same dream. Kind of strange isn't it!"

"You know the rest of the story," said Tommy.

"So, what happens now?" asked Katie.

"Well, I guess I can have someone look at the first tunnel on the left of the lost mine," responded the Sheriff. "The Deputy that found you last night seems to think you are right about finding the lost mine and graveyard. That old sign saying 'The Black Hole Gold Mine' helped him believe the story. I'll let you know if we find anything." While talking with the family, the Sheriff had picked up the dirty rock that Tommy found and was slowly turning it over in his hand. "Oh, and by the way, Tommy. That is an unusual rock you found. I think you might want a jeweler to take a look at it."

The Sheriff and Deborah left. The Sheriff took Deborah home. Katie and Tommy stayed home with their mother for the rest of the day.

George came home after work and the family had dinner together. "The Sheriff called me just before I left work," announced George. "He said he checked out your story and found Joshua's body. He has his lab people looking into the site right now. He'll let us know about the results."

"But do you believe our story?" asked Tommy.

"That's a good question, brother!" added Katie. "I don't believe daddy thinks we saw Joshua Smith's ghost. I don't believe you even believe in ghosts, do you, Daddy?"

"Don't bother your father while he is eating," scolded Tammy. "You seem to be telling the truth, whether it is believable or not. I know I don't believe in ghosts, but then I can't figure out how you knew about Joshua?"

"I am afraid that we must either believe the entire story, or none of the story," stated George. "Since everything else is true, I guess I believe Deborah and the children."

On Thursday morning, Tommy got his mother to take him and Katie to a jewelry shop. He showed the jeweler the dirty piece of glass he had found.

"This isn't ordinary glass!" remarked the Jeweler. "It's an uncut diamond. It could be worthy thousands of dollars. I would like to send it to a friend of mine for a better evaluation."

"Well, I guess that will be all right," agreed Tammy. "But what will you do with the money, Tommy?"

"I want to buy a life-sized statue of Joshua Smith," replied Tommy.

"It's to go next to the statue of Sarah Smith in the lost graveyard," added Katie.

"Can we have a statue maker talk to you about the money?" asked Tammy of the jeweler.

"I think that I can assure the statue maker that the money will be available," relied the jeweler.

On Thursday afternoon, the Sheriff called George at work. "George," stated the Sheriff, "this is the Sheriff. My lab team has found the body of Joshua Smith buried in the lost mine. They also found a knife and hatchet in Joshua's body just as Deborah described. It does look like murder. The knife and hatchet were the property of Benjamin Black and Walter Flounder."

"So, that confirms the story by Deborah, Tommy, and Katie," said George. "Everything they said was true?"

"It gets even better," added the Sheriff. "One of the lab boys took a tour of one of the other tunnels in the mine. At the end of it he found sulfur deposits in the coal seam! So, we have motive, opportunity, and method for a murder."

"Where do we go from here?" requested George.

"Well, I think we need to contact the descendants of Joshua, Benjamin and Walter," replied the Sheriff. "I know they will be interested in the lost graveyard and mine. Maybe they can tell us something more of all this."

"That's fine," agreed George. "Thank you for calling. Goodbye."

"Goodbye," said the Sheriff.

When George got home, he told everyone about what the sheriff had said. He had already called Deborah from work. Tammy told George about the diamond and the statue of Joshua.

"Now all we need are the confession letters from Benjamin and Walter," commented Tommy.

"That would mean Joshua's murderers will be found out and the spirits of Joshua and Sarah could go to their eternal reward," added Katie.

"What letters?" asked Tammy.

"You didn't mention any letters before," stated George.

"Oops!" remarked Tommy and Katie together.

"I think we need Aunties presence before we said anything more," added Tommy.

"Aren't we entitled to a lawyer?" asked Katie.

"After dinner, you two are going to your rooms. Then, I am going to talk to your Aunt!" announced George.

"Oh dear!" exclaimed Tammy. "What has Auntie been up to this time?"

So, after dinner, Katie and Tommy went to their rooms. They were to stay there until they were called. Meanwhile George telephone Deborah, and she agreed to come over to George's house.

When Deborah arrived, Katie and Tommy were allowed to come down to the living room. George requested, "Auntie, why don't you tell us about what really happened on the hike!"

"If I tell you the story, you will just say you don't believe me," begin Deborah. "What we told you about the hike was true, only we left out part of it."

"Right!" agreed Tommy. "Like about the three or four days we spent in Oz."

"And the trial of Benjamin Black and Walter Flounder for murder!" added Katie.

"I know most adults don't believe in the Land of Oz and neither did I before this happened," stated Deborah. "However, you did ask for the whole story." So Deborah told Tammy and George the whole story about the hike. Tommy and Katie helped with some of the details.

When the story was finished, all that George and Tammy could say was, "We don't believe a word of it!"

"I did warn you!" Deborah reminded them. "However, if the confession letters do turn up, how are you going to explain them?"

"I don't intend to explain anything!" commented George.

"However, it will be interesting to see if the letters do exist," added Tammy. "Anyway, I think we should forgive Deborah, Katie, and Tommy for leaving out the Oz part of the story."

"Okay!" agreed George. "You three are off the hook, for now! But don't do it again!"

On Friday afternoon, the Sheriff called George at work, once more. "You are not going to believe this," began the sheriff. "The descendants of Benjamin Black and Walter Flounder have shown me confessions stating Benjamin and Walter murdered Joshua Smith!"

"You're right," agreed George, "I don't believe it!" although he did believe it. It seems Deborah, Tommy, and Katie had taken a trip to Oz.

"Anyway," continued the Sheriff, "the descendants want to give Joshua a proper burial and publish a newspaper statement about the murder. The statement will be in this evening's paper."

When George got home, Tammy was holding the evening paper. "You better see this, George!" called Tammy. "The confession letters have surfaced, and somehow the paper got hold of the story about the diamond and Joshua's statue."

"So, I have heard," remarked George. "I guess I had better plan to take the day off so we can all go to the funeral. When is the funeral?"

"On Monday," replied Tammy.

Chapter 31
Joshua Laid to Rest

On Monday afternoon, the sun was shining and the temperature was expected to hit eighty degrees. The folks of Opossum Bottoms had gotten together and arranged a funeral for Joshua Smith. It was held in the local community church. People showed up from all over the county. There were descendants of Joshua Smith, Benjamin Black, and Walter Flounder present. Members of the press and the Sheriffs department were also in attendance. Deborah, George, Katie, Tammy, and Tommy were there.

This was the final step in getting the ghosts of Joshua and Sarah released to their eternal reward. Deborah, George, Katie, Tammy, and Tommy were only too happy to arrange for Joshua's burial. For Joshua and Sarah had been a great help to them when they needed help!

Many of the people attending the funeral were there just to meet Deborah, Katie, and Tommy. Everyone was excited about the finding of the old lost graveyard and lost mine. The finding of the lost mine could mean a chance for the community to gain some new jobs. Since the community had a lack of good jobs available for its residents, a new mine would greatly help the local economy.

There were hymns sung by everyone. Special music followed the hymn singing. The church was filled with flowers. This overdue funeral was to tie up all the loose ends of the crime which happened two-hundred years ago. It was more like a celebration, than a funeral, for it was to be the final release of two spirits to their eternal reward. They had a closed casket holding the remains of Joshua's body which had been found in the mine.

The descendants of Benjamin Black and Walter Flounder got up and apologized for the deeds of their ancestors. They also thanked Deborah, Katie, and Tommy for bringing the matter of Joshua's murder and his murderers to justice. Secretly, they now thought that they had much more interesting ancestors than they had ever imagined.

The descendants of Joshua and Sarah Smith thanked Deborah, Katie and Tommy for solving the two-hundred year-old mystery of what had happened to Joshua Smith. At least now they could finish writing that part of their family history.

"We are here to finally lie to rest, Joshua Smith!" announced the minister. "And in so doing, we will also allow the spirit of Sarah Smith to go to her eternal reward. All of us remember hearing stories about the lost graveyard and mine. It included a statue of Sarah which was said to turn its head toward the lost mine on nights of the full-moon. We now know that these stories were true. .... Now let us pray!"

The minister then prayed that Sarah and Joshua Smith might now be released to their eternal reward. He also prayed for forgiveness for those who had committed this murder, and that the wronged parties could also forgive those that committed the crime.

There was a short meal and social gathering after the service. Everyone was invited to attend it. This gave the people a chance to get better acquainted with each other. Many of the descendants of the Smiths, Blacks, and Flounders were meeting each other for the first time. It was hoped that they could all become good friends.

After this short meal, everyone was invited to go out to the lost graveyard for the internment of Joshua Smith. He was to be buried next to his wife's grave. The grave side service was very short and to the point, and concluded with Joshua being laid to rest. Joshua's old memorial marker was removed from the old graveyard. A new marker was placed at the base of where his statue would be placed. It told the story of what had happened to Joshua and how his murder was finally solved.

By the time all of this had been done, it was getting dark. Most of the people started leaving the graveyard and going on their way. Sigi, who had been kept in the car all of this time, was finally allowed to come see Joshua's grave. Soon, the only people left were Deborah, George, Katie, Tammy, and Tommy.

"I think it is time we were going," announced George. "Katie, Tommy, and Deborah, I believe you more than kept your promise to Joshua. He couldn't have had a better send off!"

"I must admit that I didn't believe your story at first," confessed Tammy. "However, you convinced the Sheriff, and got Joshua's murder solved. I will have to listen more carefully to all of you in the future."

"I have to admit that our story was not as strange as some of the tales I've heard about the Land of Oz," remarked Deborah. "Even so, it wasn't an easy job getting the Sheriff to believe us."

"And who is going to believe two children?" added Katie.

"Anyway, I now believe everything you said," replied George. "Well, maybe not everything you have said about the Land of Oz, but I believe everything you said about your hike and the mine!"

"Before we leave," suggested Deborah, "I think there are two people that want to say goodbye to us. This will give George and Tammy a chance to meet them as well."

"Auntie!" cried Katie. "You don't mean that we are going to say goodbye to Joshua and Sarah?"

"I am afraid that is just what I mean," replied Deborah. "Don't you feel their presences?"

"Are they coming as ghosts or with bodies?" asked Tommy. "I do feel a slight chill, but the temperature is still around eighty degrees."

"I feel the chill too!" agreed Katie. "And it is still warm and humid."

"We also, have a strange feeling. What is it?" asked Tammy and George together.

"Why don't we find out?" suggested Deborah. "Joshua! Sarah! Are you still here? If so, let us see you."

"Are you sure you now believe in ghosts?" asked the voice of a man.

"Right!" added the voice of a woman. "If ghosts don't exist, then none of this ever happened!"

"Very funny!" called Deborah. "I believe we said that when you were trying to haunt us. However, since ghosts don't exist, and we weren't able to help out Joshua, we must not be having this discussion. Come on everyone, let's leave!"

"All right, you win!" stated Joshua. "Here I am. Now do George and Tammy believe in me?" With that, Joshua lit up his ghostly image for all to see it. Of course it showed the knife in his back and the hatchet in his head.

"Well! That isss ahha," stuttered a startled George. "You are scary!"

"Oh, cut it out George!" scolded Tammy. "If these ghosts helped Katie and Tommy, then I am willing to believe in them. They don't scare me! Well, not much!"

"Good!" said Sarah, as she appeared next to Joshua. "We wanted to say goodbye to Deborah, Katie, Tommy, Sigi, and Rocky before we left forever."

"But where's Rocky?" asked Joshua. "After all, he did help you find the mine."

"Arf!" barked Sigi, and looked toward the entrance to the mine.

Just at that instant, Rocky came out of the mine and joined the group.

"Well, at least Rocky has sense enough to stay away from most people," remarked Deborah.

"Now that we are all here!" announced Sarah, "I want to thank each of you for helping out Joshua and me. Without the help of Deborah, George, Katie, Tammy, Tommy, Rocky, and Sigi, we would still be two separate ghosts that didn't even know about the other ghost's problem."

"Yes!" added Joshua. "We owe you all a great debt! You have given us much happiness. You cannot imagine how little hope there was for us. Why would anyone ever look for the lost mine? And if they did, why should they care about Joshua's murder?"

"I must say that your method for solving our problem was most unique!" commented Sarah. "Thank you for all your help!"

"Yes!" added Joshua. "Thank you for everything."

"Now we must really be going," stated Joshua.

"And I am happy to say, we will not be back!" added Sarah, "Goodbye everyone."

"And thank you, once again!" called Joshua. 'We are off to our eternal reward."

Sarah and Joshua took hold of each other's hands and floated up and away. Soon they were out of sight.

"Well, Deborah!" remarked George. "If I hadn't seen them for myself, I wouldn't have believed it. Correction! Even after seeing it for myself, I still don't believe it!"

"Didn't they make a lovely couple?" sighed Tammy.

"Okay, everyone," stated Deborah. "Our work is done here. Let's go home."

With that, Sigi barked goodbye to Rocky. Rocky hissed goodbye to everyone and ran back into the mine. Finally, everyone got into Georges four-wheel drive car and went home, wondering what new adventures they might face.